Lit Crit Guides

Reading and Interpreting the Works of

JANE AUSTEN

Connie Ann Kirk, PhD

Dedicated to my family and to imaginations inspired by Jane Austen

Published in 2017 by Enslow Publishing, LLC
101 W. 23rd Street, Suite 240, New York, NY 10011

Library of Congress Cataloging-in-Publication Data
Names: Kirk, Connie Ann, author.
Title: Reading and interpreting the works of Jane Austen / Connie Ann Kirk.
Description: New York, NY : Enslow Publishing, 2017. | Series: Lit Crit Guides | Includes bibliographical references and index.
Identifiers: LCCN 2015045469 | ISBN 9780766079113 (library bound)
Subjects: LCSH: Austen, Jane, 1775-1817—Criticism and interpretation—Juvenile literature. | Austen, Jane, 1775-1817—Criticism and interpretation—Handbooks, manuals, etc.
Classification: LCC PR4037 .K57 2017 | DDC 823/.7--dc23
LC record available at http://lccn.loc.gov/2015045469

Printed in the United States of America

To Our Readers: We have done our best to make sure all website addresses in this book were active and appropriate when we went to press. However, the author and the publisher have no control over and assume no liability for the material available on those websites or on any websites they may link to. Any comments or suggestions can be sent by e-mail to customerservice@enslow.com.

Portions of this book originally appeared in *A Student's Guide to Jane Austen.*

Photo Credits: Cover, p. 3 Stock Montage/Archive Photos/Getty Images; vectorgraphics/Shutterstock.com (series logo); p. 6 Universal History Archive/UIG/Getty Images; p. 12 King George III (1738–1820) (oil on canvas), West, Benjamin (1738–1820) / © Philadelphia History Museum at the Atwater Kent/Courtesy of Historical Society of Pennsylvania Collection/Bridgeman Images; p. 17 Heritage Images/Getty Images; p. 19 DEA/M. SEEMULLER/Getty Images; p. 21 Thomas Wilson's *Correct Method of German and French Waltzing*/ Wikimedia Commons/Waltz1816 72.jpg/public domain; p. 27 UniversalImagesGroup/Getty Images; p. 30 Cassell's *Old and New Edinburgh*, Vol. 1, by James Grant/Wikimedia Commons/Edinburgh Castle pre-1573.PNG/CC BY-SA 2.5; p. 33 Culture Club/Getty Images; p. 39 GL Archive/Alamy Stock Photo; p. 41 Time Life Pictures/Getty Images; p. 46 Neil McAllister/Alamy Stock Photo; p. 48 The Crescent, detail of the street, from 'Bath Illustrated by a Series of Views', engraved by John Hill (1770–1850) pub. by William Miller, 1804 (aquatint) (detail of 92988), Nattes, John Claude (c.1765–1822) (after)/Private Collection/The Stapleton Collection/Bridgeman Images; p. 51 Bas-Photo/Shutterstock.com; p. 54 Derek Croucher/Alamy Stock Photo; pp. 59, 107 Culture Club/Getty Images; p. 61 Hulton Archive/Getty Images; p. 63 Hugh Thomson/Wikimedia Commons/Thomson-PP05.jpg/public domain; pp. 68, 84 Moviestore Collection Ltd/Alamy Stock Photo; p. 71 AF archive/Alamy Stock Photo; p. 76 Cj1340/Wikimedia Commons/Cottesbrooke Hall Northamptonshire.jpg/public domain; p. 81 Hugh Thomson/Wikimedia Commons/Thomson-MP-ch48.JPG/public domain; p. 88 Library of Congress; p. 91 Emma l'entremetteuse de Douglas McGrath avec Gwyneth Paltrow 1996 d'apres Jane Austen/Bridgeman Images; p. 95 Buyenlarge/Getty Images; p. 98 Jane Austen's village (photo)/Steventon, Hampshire, UK/ Photo © Neil Holmes/Bridgeman Images; p. 103 Print Collector/Getty Images; p. 114 Silhouette of Cassandra Austen, c.1809, Meiers, John (19th century)/ Private Collection/Bridgeman Images; p. 119 Pictorial Press Ltd/Alamy Stock Photo; p. 120 Heritage Images/ Getty Images; p. 123 Jeff Morgan 07/Alamy Stock Photo.

Contents

This portrait of Jane Austen was drawn by her sister Cassandra around 1810.

1

Working a Fine Brush on Ivory

As the youngest daughter of a minister in England, Jane Austen liked to write to amuse herself and her family. She was close to her older sister, Cassandra, who appreciated her stories. Like other women of their time and social standing, neither Jane nor her sister was expected to have an occupation outside the home to support herself. Neither of the sisters ever married. Since they did not have husbands to look after them, they depended financially all their lives on the kindness of their male relatives. As a consequence, Austen spent most of her life under the care of first her father and later her brothers and other relations. She finally experienced some degree of stability in the last decade of her life when her brothers secured for her, her mother, and her sister a home of their own called Chawton Cottage.[1]

Though she was dependent on others for her livelihood, Austen's surviving letters and fiction indicate that she remained independent in her thinking and writing. She was not a retiring, submissive sort, and neither were the main characters of her stories. Austen was a smart, lively woman, full of sharp wit and good humor. She had a keen eye for observing details and contradictions in her surroundings, but she was especially perceptive about people and human nature. She took particular delight in poking fun at the ups and downs of men and women in relationships. As she matured and witnessed story after story of her friends and relatives meeting, dating, getting engaged, and marrying, Austen's writing began to center around the intricacies of courtship. She was especially interested in observing how the courtship process worked among a small circle of family and friends who all knew one another. She once called writing so closely about this topic with so few characters a "little bit (two Inches wide) of Ivory on which I work with so fine a Brush."[2]

Among others in her educated and well-read family, her father and brother Henry (Jane's favorite) liked Austen's writing. In fact, it was through the efforts of her male relatives that her first novel, *Sense and Sensibility*, was published in 1811. Just as it was deemed improper at that time for respectable women to venture out in public alone, many people also thought it was not acceptable for their writing to appear in public in print. Consequently, Austen's first novel was published not under her own name but simply under the authorship of "A Lady." That first work proved to be a popular read among the public and opened the door for the publication of more novels to come. In her lifetime, however, none of the author's works ever appeared in print under her full real name of Jane Austen.

Writing well on her "two Inches . . . of Ivory . . . with so fine a Brush," Austen went on to become one of the most important and enduring British authors of all time. Living to only forty-one years of age, Austen made a lasting impact on world literature through her six major works, all novels. This list of novels, all of which remain in print, contains classics that have been read by millions of readers around the world for nearly two hundred years. The works are: *Sense and Sensibility* (1811); *Pride and Prejudice* (1813); *Mansfield Park* (1814); *Emma* (1815); *Northanger Abbey* (1817); and *Persuasion* (1817).

Austen's novels address the dating, or courtship, personalities, and practices in the Regency period of England, but there is a universality to the stories that makes them relevant beyond their own time and place. Moreover, closer examination by scholars shows that Austen wrote not only about manners, marriage, and money—themes that are often attributed to her—but she also used the acceptable form of the domestic novel to comment about the role of women in her society. In addition, her work helped expose the disaffected wealthy as well as the pretension of the newly wealthy, who were moving up the ladder of social class. She also experimented with the

KIPLING'S "JANEITES"

Another well-known source of the name for Austen fans, "Janeites," comes from Rudyard Kipling's short story, "The Janeites," first published in *The Storyteller* magazine in 1924.[3] The story, which was the first Kipling had written in five years, is about British World War I soldiers who read Jane Austen novels as a way of coping with the horrors of war.[4] Below are some quotes from Rudyard Kipling's story that illustrate how much the soldier characters admired their favorite author:

"'Every dam' thing about Jane is remarkable to a . . . Janeite!'"[5]

"Well, . . . it's a very select Society, an' you've got to be a Janeite in your 'eart [heart], or you won't have any success.'"[6]

"You take it from me, Brethren, there's no one to touch Jane when you're in a tight place.'"[7]

form of the novel itself, a genre in world literature that was not yet one hundred years old when she began writing.

The appeal and relevance of Austen's works have resulted in a devoted following that has grown steadily over the years. The name "Janeites" for Austen fans was first used in a preface by George Edward Bateman Saintsbury to an 1894 edition of *Pride and Prejudice*.[8] The first Janeites followed in the path of those who wanted to preserve an idealized picture of Jane Austen. Early on, Austen was portrayed as the pure and innocent daughter of a clergyman who never married nor became part of the "real world" but instead stayed home with her family, working in secret and humility on her novels. This image was fueled by early biographical accounts of Austen written by relatives Henry Austen and James Edward Austen-Leigh. Later biographers have uncovered a more realistic and complex portrait of the beloved author.

To understand better and appreciate the novels of Jane Austen, it is useful to examine the times in which she lived as well as the literary context in which she wrote.

2 The Life and Times of Georgian and Regency England

In studying an author, it is important to study his or her times and culture. This is especially true of Jane Austen, who lived in the pre-Victorian time in Great Britain known as the late Georgian and Regency period. The era encompasses the years 1793 to 1820. It begins with England's war with France in 1793 under the later years of King George III's reign. This is the same King George with whom the American colonists took umbrage. The period ends at the conclusion of King George III's son's reign as Prince Regent. The prince ascended to the throne as King George IV. The Regency period is specifically considered to be the time from 1811 to 1820. Under the Regency Act, Parliament made the Prince of Wales, Prince Regent, which effectively made him ruler of the kingdom until his father's death. This was done because King George III was deemed to be incurably insane, incapable of carrying out his reign. Historical events during the late Georgian and Regency period included the War of 1812 with the United States and the Napoleonic Wars with France.

The Regency period (a common term for the late Georgian and Regency period) was marked by a growth in population and a regaining of British economic and military power around the world after the loss of the American colonies. It was also characterized by the growth of the middle class,

The time at which Austen wrote is known as the Georgian and Regency period. The country was ruled first by King George III (pictured) and then by his son, the Prince Regent (King George IV).

increased leisure, and interest in the arts. The culture fostered by the Prince Regent's personal extravagance encouraged development in architecture, food, landscaping and gardening, fashion, and amusements, such as dances and games.

The Importance of Land in Society

During the time of Jane Austen, life among the upper middle classes in the countryside of England revolved around the

AN UNPOPULAR PRINCE

The Prince Regent was a colorful character. By his own admission, he was overly fond of wine and women. He was overweight and liked to spend money on parties, art, buildings, military pageants, and other extravagances. By the time he ascended to the throne in 1820, the people of England had lost all respect for him during his previous years as Prince Regent. He was, however, a great patron of the arts. He was a patron of architect John Nash, for example, who designed London's Regent Street and Regent's Park. He also supported the renovation of Windsor Castle led by Sir Jeffry Wyatville. Perhaps the Prince Regent's most visible legacy, however, can be seen in the town of Brighton. After he visited the seaside town in 1783, he went back many times. By the end of his reign in 1827, he had sponsored several projects resulting in terraces and parks still visible throughout the town. Most notable was the construction of the grand Royal Pavilion, built in the Indian style and containing Chinese interior decorations.[1]

The Prince Regent was said to be a fan of Austen's works, reportedly keeping a set in each of his homes. The same cannot be said of Austen, who wrote in at least one letter that she "hated" the man.[2]

manors and households of affluent country gentlemen. Wealthy families owned hundreds of acres of land (sometimes as many as three thousand acres) with a large mansion as a focal point on the estate. Also built on the property were the homes of relatives, those who served the family, and possibly tenants, such as farmers. The estate might have contained acres of farmland as well as open land in the form of woods, fields, and streams. Sometimes certain areas of the property were dedicated as parks or hunting grounds.

The landed gentry were educated and did not perform manual labor. Their power in the community usually meant that they chose the local vicar (pastor) and oversaw that the church was well equipped and attended. They spent most of their time supervising the work of others and getting together with one another to facilitate suitable marriages and increase social connections and standing. This is the class of people featured most predominantly in Jane Austen's novels.

Acquiring and maintaining land was the way families increased wealth in nineteenth-century England. The aristocracy, who ranked above the landed gentry class, owned thousands of acres, typically 10,000 but as much as 150,000 acres or more. It is estimated that the aristocracy once held up to one fifth of all of the land in England.[3] These estates were owned by noblemen—such as dukes, earls, and barons—whose titles were inherited. Most of the men with these titles were concerned with government affairs and spent much of their time in London in the halls of Parliament. As a result, they were rarely home, spending only August through December at their country estates.

Common Customs

Men of the middle and upper classes in Regency England spent much of their time managing their positions in society. This meant meeting with other men in London to discuss business matters, much as business executives transact deals in cities today. Courting was serious "business" because a man's future wife and daughters might also provide a gain or loss to him in social rank, finances, or important connections.

SOCIETY AND RANK

In England in Jane Austen's time, one's heredity, social class, and social and economic standing were strictly defined in several levels, or ranks. Movement between ranks could be difficult to achieve other than through the institution of marriage. Members of certain ranks held certain titles.

The top rank, of course, was the royal family. Below that were the nobility, which included members with titles, such as duke and baron. Below that rank was the gentry class. The gentry class was made up of baronets and knights at the top and educated professionals, such as lawyers, doctors, and clergy, toward the bottom. The gentleman-farmer was a member of this rank. He did not have to work and made his money from those working on his estate and from investments. Beneath this rank were the tradesmen, tenant farmers who had done well (deficiencies in family lines or education separated them from the gentry class), and well-off artisans. The lowest rank was the working class—those such as servants, farmworkers, and trade apprentices. This lowest class often went by other names, such as "the peasantry," or "the commons."[4]

Marrying beneath one's social rank was risky and taboo; it was not expected that a wealthy man would marry for love alone.

Customs of etiquette at the time prescribed that a gentleman never smoked in the presence of ladies. He was always introduced to a woman, not the other way around, and lesser ranks were introduced to higher-ranked men; they did not introduce themselves. This is why Elizabeth Bennet in *Pride and Prejudice*, for example, cautions Mr. Collins, who is of lower rank, against introducing himself to his superior, Mr. Darcy. If a man met a woman walking on the street who obviously wanted to speak with him, it was the custom that he turn and walk with her rather than make her stop to talk with him. Likewise, he always took the street side of the walkway while they walked and talked, giving the woman more protection from the dust on the street or the occasional splashes of carriage wheels rolling through puddles.[5]

Most women in Regency England outwardly depended on men for their financial and social survival, yet there were strict rules about their interactions with them. A lady could not visit a gentleman by herself under any circumstances, for example, unless she was there on a business matter. She could not walk by herself unless she was on her way to church or a park early in the morning; she must always have another woman, gentleman, or servant with her. At dances, she could not dance with the same partner more than three times. At parties and other social gatherings, she should acknowledge the presence of every individual there at least once by speaking to him or her. If she did not wish to encourage someone's acquaintance, she had the right to accomplish her duty of acknowledgment through a stiff nod or a cold look.[6]

Young children in Regency England were often sent away from their mothers and families after the first few months of

Members of upper-class Regency England are shown here in fashionable dress of the early 1800s.

infancy to be raised by someone else until they could walk and talk.[7] Sometime later, they were sent away again to a boarding school for a few years of formal education. At times, large families sent one or two of their children to another relative who was financially better off. These relatives, such as an aunt or uncle, would adopt the child legally, and the child became entitled to their inheritance.

Land and family were agents of wealth and position in Regency England. Knowing this puts Austen's focus on relationships in a more sophisticated light for readers of the twenty-first century. She was not only writing about matters of the heart between a man and a woman, but she was also writing about the influence of these issues on the movement of power in society.

Parties, Balls, and Other Social Gatherings

People of the landed gentry class of Regency England did not work as people in businesses and industry do today, but instead they sought to improve their position in society through personal relationships. This helps explain the heavy emphasis on social events in Jane Austen's novels. It seems everyone in the novels is either preparing for an outing, party, or ball, attending such an event, thinking about or discussing the most recent social event, or anticipating or dreading the next one based on what happened at the gathering just gone by. Three of the most common kinds of social gatherings in this period included dinner parties, balls, and visits to country estates.[8] All of these and others are described in the scenes of Jane Austen's novels.

Like everything else at the time, dinner parties were not casual events thrown together at the last minute by a group of friends deciding to meet at someone's house for salad and pizza, as might happen today. Dinner parties had strict codes of conduct and etiquette. They were planned weeks in advance and with careful attention to details, from concerns about who would be invited to decisions about the menu that would be served and the seating arrangement of guests at the table. When guests arrived, they were led to the drawing room where they waited for all the other guests. This was not a cocktail hour—no drinks were served, and lively conversation was discouraged. However, this is where the host and hostess made their way around the room to greet everyone. Once everyone expected had arrived, a servant announced that dinner was served, and

Balls and other social gatherings were a common occurrence in Austen's time and, thus, for her characters as well.

the hostess arranged for a formal promenade to the dining room. All of the guests paraded into the room in pairs or small groups, but in the order of their social rank and position. The highest ranks, of course, went first. Frequently, the host took the highest-ranking female to the room on his arm.

At the table, men and women sat alternately. The man was expected to initiate conversation with the woman on his right. No guest spoke of or to the servants who were waiting on the table. After the main courses of the meal were finished, the tablecloth was removed and champagne and dessert were served. Following the meal, the ladies went to the drawing room for coffee and tea, and the men walked to a different room where many smoked while engaging in conversation. Eventually, the men and women mingled in the same room, where there might be singing, dancing, or some other form of entertainment. At the conclusion of the evening, carriages were called to take the guests home.[9]

A ball was a more involved affair and could include as many as two hundred to five hundred people. It featured grand decorations and an orchestra. Balls were either public or private. Public balls were held at town halls and other village places where anyone with a subscription could attend all the balls of the season (typically all winter). Private balls were held in private homes or public halls but were attended by invitation only.

The hostess sent out invitations three to six weeks in advance of a ball. A response was expected within twenty-four hours. Great care was taken with the facilities to make sure there was a place for everything. The house or hall needed a place for the orchestra, (usually farthest from the door and partially hidden by decorative plants or other decorations), a large area for dancing, somewhere to hang coats, a room for refreshments, a more private area where women might go if their dresses needed mending, and a room with tables where the older guests could play cards while the younger people danced.

Dances began by the highest-ranking male guest dancing with the hostess and/or her daughters. Kinds of dances included the minuet, the quadrille, early forms of the waltz, and many varieties of country dances. At the start of a dance, the man was supposed to bow and the lady curtsy. At the conclusion of a dance, the man escorted the woman around the room, asking her if she wanted any refreshments. If she did, he would accompany her to the room set up for that purpose

People dancing at a ball in early nineteenth-century England. Those attending the ball were expected to follow strict protocol when dancing and socializing.

where they could sample from selections of lemonade, wine, biscuits, tea, or other drinks and cakes.[10]

Balls were popular in Austen's time, and she apparently enjoyed them very much herself. She judged a good ball by the number of people who attended but especially by the numbers of couples that danced. "The ball on Thursday was a very small one indeed . . . There were but seven couples, and only twenty-seven people in the room."[11] She considered a ball where eight couples danced "poor." One where "seventeen couple(s)" danced was satisfactory. Her cousin once wrote of a ball where thirty couples danced and that could be judged nothing less than a success.[12]

Not all men who attended balls danced. Women were obliged to avoid insulting a man by refusing to dance with him unless they were prepared to sit down for the rest of the evening. Women got around this polite custom by standing near the men they wished to ask them to dance and trying to avoid those they did not favor. Sometimes, they would dance with a less than favorable partner in order to stay available for partners they desired later on. Balls were the site of more than dancing, however. At their card games, elders discussed health concerns, the old days, and potential matches among the young people.

At the balls, as with all social engagements of the day, men and women needed to negotiate their conflicting needs of love and money. Hosts and hostesses hoped to increase their social position by ensuring that everyone had a good time—manipulations involving power, position, and wealth were all going on simultaneously with affairs of the heart, both amid much flourish and grand style.

Once the winter months had passed, a third type of social engagement took place more frequently in Regency England.

The Ball: Drinking and Dancing

Negus—Concocted by Colonel Francis Negus and named after him, this drink was popular at balls during Austen's time. It consisted of a blend of sugar, water, and wine, such as port or sherry. Some recipes also contained calf's foot jelly, lemon juice, and spices.[13]

Quadrille—The quadrille was a popular dance at balls in Austen's time and was frequently the first dance of the evening. Something like a square dance in slow motion, the quadrille featured four couples dancing in a diamond-shape pattern.

Country Dances—Frequently, balls featured many kinds of country dances where men lined up on one side and women on the other. Movements in and out of line were called heys. "Hands across figures" involved small groups of two couples forming a circle by joining their right hands then turning half a revolution one way and then back the other. Some dances involved couples moving down the line, performing steps while the dancers at the end of the line waited. During this waiting, couples could engage in conversation or flirting. Some of these dances could take a half hour or hour to complete their way down the line.[14]

Travel and visits to country houses became popular during better weather when carriages could roll more swiftly and people could enjoy the scenery along the way. Because travel took so long, visits tended to last for some time; visits of weeks or even months in duration were not uncommon. During these visits, men typically rose early in the morning and went hunting, fishing, or shooting during the day. Women, by contrast, slept in late, often until 10:30 a.m. They typically occupied themselves with needlework, walking around the gardens and grounds, playing music, painting, or writing long letters. Frequently, hosts and hostesses arranged day outings when visitors took short drives in carriages to see some site in the neighborhood. The days ended with dinner, which was organized much as a dinner party, followed by men in the smoking room and women in the drawing room, then getting together for light games, such as cards or charades before bed.[15]

Social functions such as dinner parties, balls, and visits to country estates served an integral function among landed gentry society in the Regency period. Not only did they provide a social outlet for families living in the countryside, but they also established and reaffirmed connections that were important to the economy and growth of the region.

3 Literature in Austen's Time

Though it is difficult to think this way now, the novel was a fairly new art form in Jane Austen's day. Unlike poetry and plays, which have been around for thousands of years—since the time of the ancient Greeks—the novel was not quite a century old when Austen began writing in the form. Her six major works are all novels. Arguably, one of the most lasting contributions Austen made to world literature was to take the traditional forms the novel had become before her time and expand the function and form of what the novel itself could do.

Daniel Defoe's *Robinson Crusoe*, or *The Life and Strange Surprising Adventures of Robinson Crusoe*, published in 1719, is frequently named by scholars as one of the first complete novels recognizable as such in English. In this story, a man must make do for himself on an island after a shipwreck. He does so by learning to use plants, wildlife, and his British resourcefulness, as well as enlisting the help of a native islander. Jonathan Swift's *Gulliver's Travels*, published in 1726, follows the adventure story format of *Robinson Crusoe* but adds a layer of satire that criticizes British life of the day. In England, the novel evolved from these adventure stories and other forms.

Different classifications, or genres, of the novel developed as fiction writers found new ways to write longer narratives. Some of these traditional forms include the picaresque, gothic, epistolary, and domestic novels. Austen uses elements of

Who Jane Read

Through her letters, references to books that characters in her novels read, and other sources, scholars have determined that two of Austen's favorite authors were critic, biographer, poet, essayist, and lexicographer Samuel Johnson (1709–1784), also known as Dr. Johnson, and William Cowper (1731–1800), an eighteenth-century poet and letter writer. Others included Frances (Fanny) Burney d'Arblay (1752–1840) and Maria Edgeworth (1767–1849).

each of these forms in her work in unique ways. Her stories, however, represent the best that the fiction form of literature has to offer—that which defies classification.

Picaresque Novel

Not to be confused with "pic*ture*sque," which means visually appealing, "picaresque" comes from the Spanish word *picaro*, for rogue or rascal. The picaresque novel began as interrelated stories in Spain but developed more fully in the novel form in England. It features a rogue who gets by on his charm and wits through one adventure after another. Examples of this type of novel are *Moll Flanders* by Daniel Defoe, published in 1722, and *The History of Tom Jones, A Foundling* by Henry Fielding (1749).[1] Austen was familiar with this form, though she did not use it in her major works. Evidence does exist, however, that she experimented with picaresque elements in her juvenilia (childhood writing).

Gothic Novel

The gothic novel derives its name from the Gothic architecture of many of its principal settings, such as castles. The form, developed in the eighteenth century, is characterized by

Samuel Johnson was one of Austen's favorite writers. His works included biographies, essays, poetry, and letters.

mystery and strangeness. It can be macabre. Typically, a young innocent woman is threatened by an older, more experienced male authority figure, perhaps a relative or other caretaker. The woman is often hidden away as a prisoner and locked up in spooky places, such as an attic, tower, dungeon, or ruin. Her sexual innocence is threatened by the bad male character, and a good male character goes on several adventures in a quest to rescue her. If the hero succeeds, he marries her with her innocence intact; if he fails, the woman dies. Conclusions of classic gothic novels rarely deviate from these two scenarios.

The earliest gothic novel in English is said to be *Castle of Otranto* by Horace Walpole, published in 1764.[2] Austen and her family were more familiar with the gothic novels of Ann Radcliffe, which were popular in Austen's time early in the nineteenth century. Radcliffe's gothic novels include *The Castles of Athlin and Dunbayne* (1789), *A Sicilian Romance* (1790), *The Romance of the Forest* (1791), *The Mysteries of Udolpho* (1794), and *The Italian* (1797).

Though Austen did not write gothic novels, she did incorporate elements of the gothic into her fiction, particularly in *Northanger Abbey*. In that novel, Catherine Morland faces threats to her innocence from the Tilney family. Catherine is not an ordinary gothic figure, however, and the distinction is important. Rather than set the novel in another time and place, Austen places the action squarely in her own contemporary time period in early nineteenth-century England. In addition, while the women in Austen's fiction often face economic hardship from their limited prospects of making a living, they are not helpless prisoners but are more empowered to make choices about what will happen to them.

Epistolary Novel

An epistle is a letter, so the epistolary novel is one that is written in the form of correspondence between characters. Given that the people living in the early part of the nineteenth century did not have telephones or e-mail and instead wrote lengthy letters on a regular basis to keep in touch with one another, it is perhaps natural that this form should be attempted as a means of telling long stories. The epistolary novel of the period was frequently written as though the chapters were letters between women.

Early examples of epistolary novels in English include *Pamela; or, Virtue Rewarded* by Samuel Richardson (1740) and two others of Richardson's works, *Clarissa Harlowe* (1747–1748) and *The History of Sir Charles Grandison* (1753–1754).[3] Austen is said to have thought especially highly of *History*, even to the point of considering it her favorite novel.

juvenilia

Works written by an author when he or she was a child.

Scholars have determined that the first drafts of both *Pride and Prejudice* and *Sense and Sensibility* were written in epistolary form. Clearly, something about the form appealed to Austen. In *Northanger Abbey*, her character Henry Tilney speaks about letter writing directly, commenting on the differences between letters written by men and those by women. In a minor work, *Lady Susan*, Austen demonstrates her skill at sustaining a story through the epistolary form. For her major works, however, she eventually reworked her stories so that they were told from the point of view of an outside narrator.

Writing in 1939, the widely respected Austen scholar Mary Lascelles explains why she thinks Austen changed her narrative strategy from the epistolary technique to a third-person point of view:

> Point of view, in fact, may mean position rather than vision; and . . . Jane Austen . . . habitually establishes the heroine's position as the point of view for the story . . . Here lies, I believe, at least a partial explanation

The castle is a common setting for many gothic novels. Austen includes some aspects of the gothic novel in *Northanger Abbey*.

> of Jane Austen's relinquishment of the novel-in-letters: in that form, however constant the vision position (the moral and emotional point of view) may remain, the position (the point of vantage from which people and happenings are described) must shift for every correspondent.[4]

In other words, Lascelles theorizes that Austen discovered that the vantage point of the narrator telling the story should stay consistent in order to keep the focus of the story on her heroine. She wants the reader's attention to be on the characters, not on the narrator.

Domestic Novel

British novels of the 1700s and 1800s were frequently domestic novels—that is, those with settings in the home and with female characters whose concerns revolve around home and family. These works did not feature depictions of business or the world away from the hearth. Though Austen's novels certainly do focus on the home and on relationships, they differ from domestic novels in that they also address other matters and depict other aspects of nineteenth-century life.

Rather than be isolated completely in the home sewing or tending to the family and its needs, women in Austen's novels are clearly part of society. Relationships extend beyond the family to friends and new acquaintances. Events in the stories take women away from home to become an integral part of social functions that require skills beyond what is needed in the domestic sphere within one's family.

Austen writes about the time of life when women were between being dutiful daughters and faithful wives—perhaps this is the time when they are most independent, then and now. In addition, Austen describes male characters conducting business and other dealings that are not described in domestic novels. For example, Mr. Knightley discusses his farm in *Emma*. In *Pride and Prejudice*, Mr. Darcy helps Mr. Bennet and Mr. Gardiner make an arrangement with Wickham to save Lydia Bennet's reputation.

Austen uses aspects of the domestic novel form with which she was familiar to expand her stories beyond the confines of the walls of the private home. Her works tend to focus on the social arenas where power was bought and sold in the form of matchmaking and marriages in the country society of Regency England.

Realistic Fiction

Jane Austen has been called one of the first realist novelists in the English language. Realism in fiction developed in the early nineteenth century. Writing realistically means that rather than set her stories in exotic places, such as islands where she had never visited and in times long before when she lived, Austen sets her novels in the "here and now" of her own time and place.

Austen also writes about characters that could live in her own household or next door—in other words, she writes about what she knows firsthand. At the time, this made her work instantly recognizable to her readers because it was accurate and represented or mirrored reality as she knew it to be.

realistic fiction

A story that portrays setting, characters, and plots that could actually exist in the world. It is the opposite of fantasy, which is a partly or completely imagined world that is not bound by rules of reality.

For example, Austen alludes to books her readers would have read and places they may have gone in England. She refers to other events in the world, such as slavery in the

Austen's novels commonly show women traveling, by carriage or by foot, often for social purposes.

West Indies, from the perspective of someone like herself who had never been there but who had heard about it from those who had.

Austen once gave writing advice to her niece, Anna, who was attempting to write a novel: "[Y]ou had better not leave England. Let the Portmans [Anna's characters] go to Ireland, but as you know nothing of the Manners there, you had better not go with them. You will be in danger of giving false representations. Stick to Bath & the Foresters. There you will be quite at home."[5]

Through this advice, Austen is telling her niece that the narrative should say that the Portmans went to Ireland, but she should not take the reader there and attempt to portray a scene in Ireland. Since she had never been there herself, she would not be able to depict Ireland's "Manners" accurately, or in a realistic light.

Narration and Point of View

Point of view in fiction is the perspective from which a story is told. With a first-person point of view, the story is told by a character within the story. Readers identify a first-person point of view by the use of "I" as in "I danced at the ball." Jane Austen uses a third-person point of view in all six of her major novels. This means that a narrator outside the action tells the story. This viewpoint uses third-person pronouns, such as "she" and "he," as in "She danced at the ball."

Though the third-person narrator is frequently associated with the author in the reader's mind, in fact the narrator may be another of the author's creations. The narrator is not a character but rather a "voice" existing outside the story that the author has created to tell the tale.

Austen as Storyteller

exposition

The descriptions of places, people, events, and movements in the story or novel through the voice of the narrator.

dialogue

The characters' direct speech, noted in the text by quotation marks.

While Austen preferred to keep her canvas small on which to paint her miniatures of everyday life in the country, she was not overly concerned with description as a whole. One of the reasons why her novels may enjoy such a wide range of readership is that her plots move forward rapidly with strong, witty dialogue and relatively little exposition (background or narration).

Literary critic John F. Burrows claims that Austen's use of exposition "comprises only about three-fifths of the words used in her six novels and, in *Emma*, only a trifle over half." He argues, "One reason why she can afford to leave much unsaid is that, when they were written, her novels were so immediate in time and place."[6] Readers in Austen's time understood references to popular books, places in England, and other references of the day. She does not, for example, spend a lot of time explaining how the women's dresses looked at balls or what each room in the grand manor houses on the country estates looked like. Instead, she takes her characters to these places and gets them talking and moving. This keeps the action of the plot moving forward as well. The reader becomes part of the story in an immediate way by relating directly with the characters and not sitting on the sidelines, as it were, with narration serving as a kind of filter between the reader and the action. This technique makes the stories, written nearly two hundred years ago, still seem fresh today. This may also help explain why all of Austen's

Free Indirect Discourse

A particular stylistic technique that Austen is often credited with perfecting is called free indirect discourse, or FID. FID is used with a third-person point of view to shorten the perceived distance between the narrator and a character.

Below are examples of sentences that show the differences between direct discourse, indirect discourse, and FID. Notice how the narrator and the character appear to merge in the FID form:

> Indirect discourse—She thought she would visit her cousin the next day.
>
> Direct discourse—She thought, "I will visit my cousin tomorrow."
>
> Free indirect discourse (FID)—She would visit her cousin tomorrow.

novels have been so attractive to filmmakers, since film relies on dialogue and action, rather than narration, to tell a story.

In the FID narrative technique, the narrator seems to be inside the mind of the character. The effect on the narrative is that the narrator and the character become barely distinguishable. The reader is allowed a closer look at the character's thoughts and senses while at the same time keeping a narrative distance that would not be possible with a first-person point of view. For example, a first-person point of view in the example shown would read: "I will visit my cousin tomorrow." The result is that the reader has heightened sympathy and empathy for the character, since he or she is brought closer to the character's thoughts and feelings. However, the narrator of the story maintains control and a sense of objectivity over the story.

Austen moved in and out of various techniques within individual novels to achieve desired effects. One of the most outstanding overall effects is that much of Austen's work dramatizes a segment of British society in a way that shows how individuals in that society perceived one another at the time.

4 An Unsettled Life

While some writers travel to do research, meet with people, or visit places related to their work, many authors do much of their actual writing at home. Jane Austen was among these. As people who dream up stories and shepherd their characters through various trials and triumphs, stability at home aids writers by allowing them to experience peace and quiet. It also, of course, aids in the intense concentration needed for writing well. Some writers these days enjoy working in cafés or coffee shops, malls, or outside in natural settings, but Austen was among those who preferred writing at home. This is why looking at where she lived when, in relation to her work, can be informative and interesting. Unfortunately, she did not always have the stability in her workplace that she needed on a consistent basis.

Austen's life may be divided into three major periods—times that are separated among biographers according to where she lived and who provided for her basic needs: her young years at Steventon, Hampshire, where she grew up under the care of her father (1775–1801); in Bath and elsewhere, staying with relatives after her father died (1801–1809); and in Chawton at Chawton Cottage, where she lived with her mother and sister in a home secured by her brothers (1809–1817).[1]

Growing Up at Steventon

Jane Austen was born on December 16, 1775, to Reverend George Austen and Cassandra Leigh Austen. She joined an already large family of four brothers—James, George, Edward, Henry—and one sister, Cassandra. Two other brothers, Francis and Charles, would be born after her. In a houseful of boys, it is perhaps natural that Cassandra would take immediately to her little sister. The two were lifelong friends.

As was the custom at the time among some people of their class with large families, the Austens sent little Jane away (probably at about three months of age) to be raised by a woman in the village until Jane could walk and talk. The thinking at the time (cruel as it may sound today) was that children were not impressionable as babies and could be raised by virtually any caring adult until the child reached the age of a toddler. Some biographers see the markings of this early separation in Austen's writing. Biographer Claire Tomalin, for

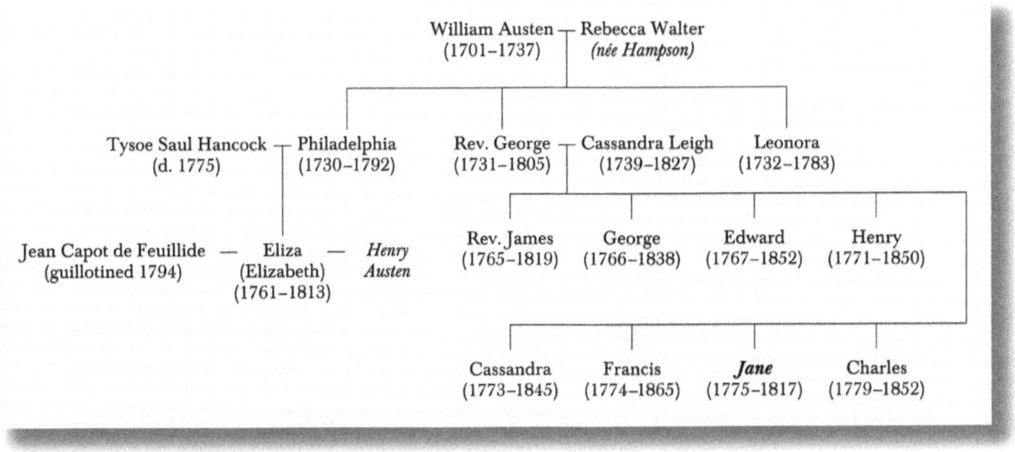

Jane Austen's family tree details her extended family on her father's side.

example, believes Austen's letters show a defensiveness and coldness that may harken back to her separation from her mother as an infant. Tomalin writes that Austen's letters "are the letters of someone who does not open her heart; and in the adult who avoids intimacy you sense the child who was uncertain where to expect love or to look for security, and armoured herself against rejection."[2] Even as this practice did take place, the Austens were said to visit the village where Jane was every day and frequently brought her back to the rectory for visits. Strangely, there is no record of the name of the village woman who cared for Jane during this time.

The same year that Charles was born, 1779, Austen's eldest brother, James, left home for St. John's College at Oxford at the young age of fourteen. At Easter 1783, at the age of seven, Jane and her sister, age ten, along with their cousin, Jane Cooper, were sent away from home again to be tutored by Mrs. Ann Cawley at Oxford. In the summer of that year, the Austen girls were exposed to typhus, and Jane nearly died. Mrs. Cawley died that October.

While they were home, the Austen girls were most likely taught by Mrs. Austen, despite the toll of doing this while managing a lively and large household. Austen's books that survive from these years include *The History of Little Goody Two-Shoes* and *Fables Choisies*. The latter is a French textbook given to her on December 5, 1783. Other surviving books include a literary anthology, *Elegant Extracts*, and a gift from her brother Edward, by Dr. Percival, *A Father's Instructions to his Children, consisting of Tales, Fables and Reflections; designed to promote the love of virtue, a taste for knowledge, and an early acquaintance with the works of Nature.*[3]

In addition to being well-read, the Austens enjoyed putting on family theatricals. In the summer of 1784, for example,

Austen grew up in this home in Steventon, a village in Hampshire, England. It was here that she wrote her first three novels.

they performed a modern comedy called *The Rivals*. By then, the shows were put on in the family barn (earlier plays were acted out in the dining room), often with cousins and friends asked to join the cast. Later, Austen would use a similar family production as a central plot point in *Mansfield Park*.[4]

By spring 1785, Jane and Cassandra were sent away again to school, this time to the Abbey House School in Reading. There they were instructed by Miss Pitts and Mme. La Tournelle (who took a French name, since she taught that language, though her real name was Sarah Hackitt). They took lessons in writing, simple mathematics, French, spelling, geography and history, needlework, drawing, music, and dancing. Though they could have stayed at the school on into their teens, the girls went home at the end of 1786 when Jane was eleven, probably because their parents thought the cost of tuition was too high. Neither Jane nor her sister ever had any other formal education after that. They also never left their immediate family surroundings again.

Though her formal schooling had ended, Jane had full access to her father's large and growing library. Mr. Austen bought books and encouraged his children to read them. There was also a boys' school held at the rectory, which meant that textbooks were part of the library. By 1801, Reverend Austen had a library of some five hundred volumes.[5]

By all accounts, Jane made use of her father's library by reading with a vengeance. She read literature, history, and works in other languages, such as Latin and Italian. Among the titles that she references in her writing or that bear her signature or other evidence of her reading are *Tom Jones* by Henry Fielding; Samuel Richardson's *Sir Charles Grandison*; Samuel Johnson's *Rasselas*; William Hayley's *Poems and Plays*; Thomas Pote's *Eton Latin Grammar;* Signor Veneroni's *The Complete*

Italian Master; Oliver Goldsmith's four-volume *The History of England, from the earliest times to the death of George II*; John Whitaker's *Mary Queen of Scots Vindicated*; and Vicesimus Knox's *Elegant Extracts*. In addition, Jane's works show familiarity with Shakespeare and British poets, such as John Milton, Alexander Pope, Thomas Gray, and William Collins.[6]

The Austen household was lively with energetic young men, including all of Jane's brothers who were still at home, as well as her father's students. Most biographers conjecture that Jane and Cassandra both benefited from the education the boys were receiving. Discussions, books, and family theatricals were shared and enjoyed among them all. Writer Carol Shields points out in her biography of Austen that what is perhaps most important to consider about Austen's family and her work is that "all the family read novels . . . [when] the novel as a form was in its infancy."[7] Apparently, they were fairly indiscriminate in their taste at the time. They read everything from romance novels to more serious literature.

About 1787, Austen started writing. Her father encouraged her efforts, and she frequently read what she wrote to her family for their entertainment and feedback. She wrote so much that she collected her early writing into three notebooks. She wrote histories and prayers, novelettes and sketches, verse, letters, and other things. Among her more frequent kinds of pieces were short, epistolary novels.

Carol Shields notes that Austen's juvenilia shows "the sometimes painful process of educating herself to become a writer."[8] As the youngest daughter in a family of so many boys, her father's approval must have been important to her. A clue to the warmth of his support can be seen in his dedication to one of the notebooks he purchased for her: "Effusions of Fancy/by a very Young Lady/Consisting of Tales/in a Style entirely new."[9] Shields also observes that Austen's juvenilia is different from that of other world-renowned authors in that it was fairly public (since she often read from it to her family) and that it was "part of a continuum."[10] Austen drafted *Pride and Prejudice* at the young age of twenty-one, only a few short years after she was writing her early efforts in her notebooks as a teenager.

Even as Austen enjoyed her days reading and writing and sharing her work with her family by the hearth, the idyllic family scene around her was beginning to change. Older siblings were growing up and moving out. Her brothers were going to college or joining the clergy. They were beginning to go out and establish themselves in the outside world. Edward inherited land and became a member of the landed gentry. With so many of their brothers moving on in life, it must have become painfully obvious in short order that Jane and her sister had no such choices or opportunities.

While the family at home got smaller, Jane and Cassandra cultivated more friendships and visited and entertained other relatives. It was from these interactions that Cassandra met clergyman Tom Fowle and became engaged to him in 1792. It is interesting to note that about six months after her sister's engagement, Jane wrote the last of the juvenilia that survives in her notebooks. Her next project was the minor work *Lady Susan*, probably begun in the fall of 1794. Perhaps to encourage her writing at a time when his sons were off seeking various occupations, her father bought Jane a portable leather and mahogany writing desk for her nineteenth birthday. The desk still survives. Perhaps the world owes Mr. Austen a debt of gratitude for this simple gesture, for on that desk was to be produced some of the most lasting and enjoyable literature the world would come to know.

Biographers believe Austen began writing *Elinor and Marianne*, or what would later be titled *Sense and Sensibility*, in 1795. That same year, as well, Reverend Tom Fowle joined Lord Craven's sailing party as his private chaplain and sailed off for the West Indies. While he was away in 1795, Cassandra must have enjoyed hearing of Jane's attraction for Tom Lefroy, a young Irish lawyer she met that year and whom many say may have been the love of her life.

While Cassandra waited for her fiancé to return from the sea and prepared for marriage, Jane's relationship with Tom Lefroy started to develop, only to be squashed by his relatives before it could bloom. In early 1796, Lefroy was sent away to London before his attachment to the lower-ranked Jane Austen could develop any further. Perhaps her writing desk provided solace during these confusing times. Scholars believe that in October of that year, Austen began a manuscript called *First Impressions* that would eventually become *Pride and Prejudice*.

In February 1797, Tom Fowle died of fever in San Domingo. Cassandra was crushed and went into what amounted to a surrogate widowhood. She did not seek out other romantic prospects and never married. This loss, combined with Jane's loss of Tom Lefroy to his family's preferences, resulted in the sisters bonding in a special way. They seemed to resign themselves to staying home and caring for their parents and each other or going out as they were needed to help with their brothers' growing families. Cassandra, in particular, seemed to age prematurely and gravitate toward a maidenly aunt role. Her visits to Edward's household, in particular for this purpose, sent her away from home, resulting in many of the surviving letters from Jane to her.

This twelfth-century church where Jane's father was a rector still stands today.

Mr. Austen continued to support Jane's writing. In November 1797, he wrote a letter to publisher Thomas Cadell in London inquiring about publishing what was, at that time, *First Impressions*. He clearly wanted to help his daughter, but it is not impossible that he may have had finances at least somewhat in mind as well. He had given up the school by this time, and his farm income was low. If he did not expect Jane to bring in any money from her book, he seemed at least to want assurance that the project would not be too costly to publish at the author's expense. In his letter, he did not mention who wrote the manuscript or anything about what it was about. The letter was sent back, rejected, by return post.[11]

By late 1800, Austen faced another shake-up to her home life that had come to mean so much to her. Mr. Austen decided to retire from the rectory and move himself, his wife, and two adult daughters to Bath. There is some suggestion that he hoped the big change might help his daughters find husbands.

Bath: Insecurity and Upheaval

The years at Bath are striking in Jane Austen's life for how different they were from what went before and what occurred afterward. After the family moved there, Austen's pen went virtually silent. She became part of the social circles she wrote about, attending balls and other social gatherings. She was not without marriage prospects while in Bath. One gentleman, Harris Bigg Wither, proposed to her on December 2, 1802. At first, Austen accepted his proposal, but she changed her mind the next morning. That same year, she revised *Susan* (later titled *Northanger Abbey*) and sold it to Crosby and Co. of London, who held on to the manuscript but never published it. She may have also drafted a minor work, *The Watsons*, in 1804.

The spring waters in Bath were said to have a restorative effect, and many people visited the town seeking a cure for their health problems.

When her father died in January 1805, the event represented more than a crushing emotional blow. It effectively set Austen's mother, sister, and herself adrift. They went from one family residence to another, staying with relatives with no real home of their own. Austen's older brother, James, had moved into the Steventon house, so that was not an option for them. Since they had not inherited or married into property, the three women were at a loss. Austen's brothers tried to provide some money for them and temporary housing. The years passed by with their going virtually house to house, continually changing residences and enduring the insecurity of constant upheaval and living solely on the good graces of relatives.

Finally, in 1809, Jane's brother Edward secured his mother and sisters permanent housing in Chawton, and they moved there in July. At thirty-three, Jane Austen's years of growing and wandering had ended. She was about to embark on her fullest period of creativity.

A New Life in Chawton

The move to the L-shaped brick house called Chawton Cottage began a major shift in Austen's ability to write. The house was a ten-minute walk to the village, where about sixty families lived, mostly laborers on Edward's farms and property. Biographer Claire Tomalin observes: "The effect on Jane of this move to a permanent home in which she was able to re-establish her own rhythm of work was dramatic. It was as though she were restored to herself, to her imagination, to all her powers: a black cloud had lifted. Almost at once she began to work again. *Sense and Sensibility* was taken out, and revision began."[12]

Indeed, though she had drafted early versions of *Sense and Sensibility*, *Pride and Prejudice*, and *Northanger Abbey* before she arrived at Chawton, it was the Chawton years that picked back up where the Steventon years had left off in terms of Austen's creativity and output. By the winter of 1810, Austen had sold *Sense and Sensibility*, and it was published the following year. Its sale no doubt encouraged her to begin an entirely new work, *Mansfield Park*. At the same time, she revised *First Impressions* into *Pride and Prejudice* and sold it in late 1812. It was published in early 1813. In mid-1813, she completed *Mansfield Park* and probably sold it late in the year. In January 1814, she started writing *Emma*, and on May 9, *Mansfield Park* was published. In August of 1815, Austen started writing *Persuasion*, and in December of that year *Emma* was published. By July of 1816, Austen had completed *Persuasion*. In early 1817, she began work on another new novel, *Sanditon*. That novel, however, was cut short not from lack of creativity or will, but because Austen's short life did not allow her to complete it.

It was as though the dams had burst when Austen moved into Chawton Cottage. Her beloved Steventon was only seventeen miles away. The six bedrooms in the cottage allowed for

Austen in Bath

As the name suggests, there were and are public baths in Bath, England. In Austen's time, the town was second only to London in size. It was a resort town used by the wealthy. Austen visited there when she was young, but it was most likely not quite as pleasurable being a resident of a resort town as it was being one of its many visitors. Austen set part of Northanger Abbey there.[13]

Austen lived here at Chawton Cottage, along with her mother and sisters, for the last years of her life.

re-gatherings of the family—brothers and their wives and children—so that, at times, it must have brought back memories of their lively household at Steventon.

Henry visited with friends from London; Jane's other brothers, who were officers in the navy, visited when they were home from sea. Edward stayed there and also at Chawton House, the Elizabethan manor nearby that he also owned. His daughter, Anna, whom Aunt Jane gave writing advice to in her letters, recalled driving on shady country lanes between the larger house and the cottage. Austen wrote a verse about the house to her brother Frank to accompany a note congratulating him on the birth of a son:

> Our Chawton home, how much we find
> Already in it, to our mind;
> And how convinced that when complete
> It will all other houses beat.[14]

For a writer who focused so much of her fiction on the domestic lives and social interactions of a few country families, settling in and feeling comfortable at Chawton Cottage must have felt like coming home.

Both the cottage itself and the larger manor, Chawton House, survive, and visitors can see where the author called home and where she wrote all of her mature work. Appropriately, it was from this house and garden that Austen's fiction was launched to the world. The first of these works was *Sense and Sensibility*. The publication of this novel would mark the beginning of a remarkable—though tragically short—literary career.

5 The First: *Sense and Sensibility*

Jane Austen's first novel, *Sense and Sensibility*, ranks with *Pride and Prejudice* and *Emma* as one of her most well-known and popular works. It is likely that Austen began writing the manuscript in 1795 when she lived under the care of her father at her childhood home at Steventon. That manuscript does not appear to have survived; however, scholars have determined that the original story was written in epistolary form, that is, in the form of letters. The book's original title was *Elinor and Marianne*. Revisions in 1797 and 1798 changed the title to its current form and, most importantly, altered its narrative strategy from epistolary to a third-person narration. Austen is thought to have completed the manuscript in 1809 and 1810 at Chawton Cottage.[1]

In the years between when she first wrote the story in letters until it was published in 1811, Austen's life changed a great deal. Her father retired, then died, and she, her mother, and her sister, Cassandra, were left in similar circumstances to Mrs. Dashwood, Elinor, and Marianne. The situation of living with relatives and visiting friends, of finally settling in Chawton Cottage, reminds readers of the Dashwoods settling at Barton Cottage.

Plot

Mr. Dashwood dies at the beginning of the novel, leaving his property to his son, John Dashwood, and John's wife, as was customary at the time. In doing so, Mr. Dashwood leaves his second wife and three daughters, Elinor, Marianne, and Margaret, without income or a place to live. Despite Mr. Dashwood's agreement with his son that he should look after this second branch of the family, John Dashwood and his wife move into Norland Park, forcing his father's second wife and daughters out of the house. As was common practice at the time, the women are invited by a distant cousin, Sir John Middleton and Lady Middleton, to rent a cottage for a low price on their property. Their new home is called Barton Cottage.

Austen's small writing table still stands in the parlor at Chawton.

WRITTEN BY "A LADY"

Austen saw *Sense and Sensibility* published anonymously under the name "A Lady." It was not considered proper in her time for respectable women to share their writing in public. Austen's next novel, *Pride and Prejudice*, was also published anonymously, this time with the convenient attribution, "By the Author of Sense and Sensibility."

Leaving Norland Park is particularly difficult for the eldest sister, Elinor, who has become attached to Edward Ferrars, John Dashwood's brother-in-law. Once settled at Barton, however, Elinor and Marianne meet wealthy yet reserved Colonel Brandon and charming, handsome John Willoughby. Willoughby picks Marianne up after she falls down a hill and twists her ankle, and he begins a visible and lively courtship of her thereafter. For her part, Marianne does not make any attempt to hide her strong feelings for this dashing young gentleman. Suddenly, however, Willoughby receives a message and leaves for London in a hurry, to the distress of Marianne.

In the meantime, the Middletons have guests, Lucy and Anne Steele, who are related to Lady Middleton's mother, Mrs. Jennings. Lucy confides in Elinor that she has been secretly engaged for four years to a Mr. Ferrars since their days together at Plymouth, where Edward went to school, and Lucy's uncle was his teacher. Elinor assumes Lucy means Robert Ferrars, Edward's brother, but is shocked to learn that she means Edward.

Mrs. Jennings takes Elinor and Marianne to London for a change of scenery as well as to provide more opportunities for them to socialize and perhaps do some matchmaking. Colonel

Brandon tells Elinor that everyone around the city has been gossiping that Willoughby will soon be engaged to Marianne. Marianne, emotional and passionate as always, spends her days waiting for word from Willoughby, which never arrives. When they finally cross paths, Willoughby acts very coldly to Marianne with no explanation. She soon sees that he is with another woman, a Miss Grey, who, unlike Marianne, has wealth and connections.

Colonel Brandon knows something about Willoughby's past and explains it to Elinor. Mrs. Jennings has also learned since their arrival that Willoughby has spent his money and is engaged to Miss Grey. Marianne has been humiliated. On her way back to Barton, the women visit friends at Cleveland. There, Marianne comes down with a dangerous fever and takes to her bed, where Elinor nurses her. In the meantime, Edward Ferrars's mother learns about his engagement to Lucy Steele and takes away his inheritance, promising it to his brother, Robert.

Back at Barton, the sisters receive word that Lucy has married Mr. Ferrars, whom they assume to be Edward. It is, in fact, Robert—Lucy has followed the money. This means that Edward is free to become engaged to Elinor. Kind Colonel Brandon, who has looked after the sisters, wins the affection of Marianne, and both sisters are married.

Characters

Elinor Dashwood is the eldest, the most logical and practical and duty-bound daughter; in short, she is the daughter with the most "sense." Marianne Dashwood is more emotional and romantic, more passionate and unpredictable; she represents the character with the most "sensibility." As readers are reminded throughout the course of the novel, however, these two women are, like people everywhere, impossible to fit into tidy labels. Elinor, as the character of "sense," suffers deeply when she believes Edward Ferrars is engaged to Lucy Steele. Marianne, the character with vibrant "sensibility," shows her practical side when she marries kind and respectable Colonel Brandon after being hurt by her passionate romance with John Willoughby.

Techniques and Themes

In her article, "*Sense and Sensibility*: The Letter, Post Factum," Mary Favret points out that this is the novel in which Jane Austen broke with her previous use of the epistolary technique and struck out on new ground in narrative style. She had used letters with *Lady Susan*, *Elinor and Marianne*, and *First Impressions*. By the time she revised *Sense and Sensibility*, clearly a different mode was at work in her writing. With the novel's publication in 1811, Favret writes that Austen "announced her victory over the constraints of the letter."[2] By not limiting herself to that format, Austen was freer to use point of view in any way she chose. Since she no longer had to keep shifting it back and forth from one correspondent to another, she could place the point of view squarely on Elinor, which she does effectively.

The title theme of logic versus emotion is perhaps the clearest one to follow and define in the novel. Author Paul Poplawski writes: "Perhaps more than with any other of Jane Austen's major works, the title here provides a fairly reliable indication of the main concerns of the novel if we look at it in straightforward terms."[3] However, he goes on to note what other scholars and critics have also pointed out, that Austen does not exactly leave her story advocating a tidy black-and-white balance between the two elements. While a balance between the two may be most desirable, Poplawski suggests that "Jane Austen . . . puts sense and sensibility into dialogue with one another throughout the novel . . . neither mode emerges as entirely superior to . . . the other or as entirely sufficient by itself."[4]

Several critics, including Mary Poovey, Gene Ruoff, and others, describe *Sense and Sensibility* as one of Austen's darkest works.[5, 6] This is especially true when contrasted with *Pride and Prejudice*, which is known for its bright and happy tone.

THE HEAD AND THE HEART

When people fall in love, they sometimes complain that it seems as though their head is in conflict with their heart. They frequently do not behave rationally or logically, and their emotions may seem to overflow with feelings of both joy and sorrow. They can become easily confused, not sure whether they should allow their actions to be led by their head or their heart.

Austen calls these two elements sense (head, logic, or common sense) and sensibility (heart, emotions, or sentimental feelings). She is a master at depicting the natural conflict between sense and sensibility in her fiction.

Sense and *sensibility* were actually terms that Austen inherited at the time of her writing. Philosophers, essayists, and poets before her had been discussing the concepts for some time. Some of these writers included Adam Smith in *Theory of Moral Sentiments* (1759), Samuel Johnson in works such as *Rambler* (1750) and *Idler* (1759), and Hannah More in *Sensibility: An Epistle to the Honourable Mrs. Boscawen* (1782).[7]

The universality and timelessness of the sense and sensibility theme is one reason why Austen's work continues to enjoy a wide readership so many years after its first publication.

An illustration from an early edition of *Sense and Sensibility* depicts the scene in which Elinor is introduced to Robert Ferrars.

SENSE AND SENSIBILITY ON THE BIG SCREEN

The Academy Award-winning British actress Emma Thompson was asked to try her hand at writing a screenplay adapting *Sense and Sensibility* to film. It took her four years and fourteen drafts to get the script just the way she wanted it. When the film was produced, it was directed by Ang Lee. It starred Thompson as Elinor Dashwood, Kate Winslet as Marianne Dashwood, Hugh Grant as Edward Ferrars, and Alan Rickman (Professor Severus Snape in the Harry Potter films) as Colonel Brandon. The film was released in theaters in 1995. For her efforts, Thompson won the Academy Award for the best adapted screenplay.[8]

Certainly the full story of Willoughby's scandalous behavior touches on aspects of early nineteenth-century life that few readers would expect the daughter of a clergyman to be aware of, yet alone write about. In a fresh approach along these lines, author Claudia Johnson interprets the male characters in the novel as Austen's commentary on the predicament that men experienced in her time. To many of them, associating with women was either an entertaining diversion while they bided their time waiting to inherit property, or it was a means to advance or maintain social standing. Johnson makes the point that in terms of using women as diversions, both Edward Ferrars (presumably with Lucy Steele) and Willoughby (with Marianne) might be charged equally guilty.[9]

tone

The writer's attitude toward her subject or audience.

When it appeared in 1811, *Sense and Sensibility* received two early, positive reviews, both with long quotations from the novel. One was in the *Critical Review* and the other in the *British Critic*.[10] Writing about the novel's early reception, biographer Jan Fergus states that no Austen family member seems to have preferred this novel over any other.[11] Fergus believes the acceptance of the novel by the publisher, probably in February 1811, most likely spurred Austen to begin work on *Mansfield Park*, her most ambitious project to date and the first of what would be considered her mature work. The first edition of *Pride and Prejudice*, her next novel to be published, sold out quickly and increased demand for *Sense and Sensibility*. Similarly, *Sense and Sensibility* is the second Austen novel many of today's readers encounter.

Mrs. Dashwood and her three daughters (left to right: Marianne, Margaret, and Elinor) are shown in the 1996 film version of *Sense and Sensibility*.

6 THE CLASSIC: *PRIDE AND PREJUDICE*

"It is a truth universally acknowledged, that a single man in possession of a good fortune, must be in want of a wife."[1] The first sentence of *Pride and Prejudice* has become one of the most famous opening lines in literature. Similarly, Austen's second novel is the one most widely recognized, even by those who know little else about the author.

The novel's opening sentence sets the ironic and comic tone for the book as well as doing its job in igniting the interest of the reader. Who is saying a wealthy man needs a wife? Is it the man? Is it the woman who seeks to become his wife? Is it parents who need to marry off a daughter so that she may have a future beyond spinsterhood in early nineteenth-century England? *Must* he want a wife, really, and is this "truth" really "universally acknowledged"?

Austen started writing her second major novel under the working title *First Impressions*, in the fall of 1796. Scholars believe that she finished the first draft in the summer of 1797 but did not begin seriously revising the manuscript, including changing the title, until several years later. Living comfortably in Chawton Cottage and most likely newly rejuvenated in her work by the publication of *Sense and Sensibility*, it is thought that Austen revised *Pride and Prejudice* in the winter of 1811–1812.

Mr. Darcy (center) snubs Elizabeth Bennett in an early scene from *Pride and Prejudice*.

Plot

Wealthy and available Mr. Charles Bingley rents a manor nearby to the Bennets. Mr. and Mrs. Bennet are the parents of five unmarried daughters—Jane, Elizabeth, Mary, Kitty, and Lydia. Mrs. Bennet is eager to increase the marriage prospects of the elder daughters, in particular, but marrying any of her daughters off would please her immensely. Mr. Bennet pays a call on Mr. Bingley, and the girls are invited to a ball that Mr. Bingley attends. At the dance, Mr. Bingley favors Jane and dances with her. His friend, Mr. Darcy, also attends the ball. He seems uncomfortable and displeased at being there. He does not dance with Elizabeth Bennet, even going so far as to utter an insult that she overhears, and this causes everyone in their party to think him arrogant and rude.

There are several other social gatherings among the Bennets, Mr. Bingley, and Mr. Darcy. Mr. Bingley becomes more and more attached to Jane. On one occasion when Jane visits Netherfield, Bingley's estate, she is caught in a rainstorm that chills her and makes her ill. She must stay on at Bingley's home for several days—a move that, according to her matchmaking mother, creates more opportunities for courtship. Elizabeth hikes the muddy fields to Netherfield in order to care for her sister, arriving with mud splattered on her dress. This does not impress Miss Bingley, Mr. Bingley's sister, who is a snob and nothing like her brother, who is kind. Miss Bingley is unhappy that her brother has taken up with the Bennets and even unhappier when she sees Mr. Darcy, whom she desires for herself, notice Elizabeth Bennet more than she would like.

Mr. Collins, a clergyman who will inherit the Bennet household, since there are no male heirs in the immediate family, is visiting the Bennets when Jane and Elizabeth return home. He takes a liking to Elizabeth, but she does not consider him anywhere near a match and refuses his proposal. Mr. Collins's pride is hurt. In the meantime, the Bennet sisters become acquainted with some young men from the militia who are in town; most notable of these is Mr. Wickham. Mr. Wickham tells Elizabeth that Mr. Darcy and he go way back—and that Darcy cheated him out of his inheritance. Elizabeth's sympathy goes out to Wickham, and her negative view of Darcy is confirmed.

In the winter, Mr. Bingley and Mr. Darcy go to London. Mrs. Bennet and her daughters fear that their prospects for matches have diminished. Mr. Collins marries Jane's friend, Charlotte Lucas, who says she must marry the foolish clergyman because she is running out of time and choices. Jane goes to London to visit friends and also hopes she might see Mr. Bingley. However, Bingley's sister is rude to her, and Charles Bingley does not appear.

It turns out that the Reverend and Charlotte Collins live near Collins's benefactor, Lady Catherine de Bourgh, who also happens to be Darcy's aunt. When Elizabeth goes there to visit Charlotte, she sees Darcy, but it is also clear that Lady Catherine has plans for Darcy to marry her daughter. In the meantime, Darcy makes several visits to the Collinses and even offers Elizabeth a marriage proposal. She refuses, however, citing his cruel way of encouraging Bingley away from her sister Jane and revealing that she knows all about his poor treatment of Wickham. Darcy leaves, but before he does, he writes Elizabeth a letter. In the letter, he tells her that he did encourage Bingley to move on from Jane but only because he thought Jane did not seriously care for him. Wickham's story, he informs her, is a lie. In fact, Wickham is a chronic liar. He ran into bad straits when he tried to elope with Darcy's younger sister, Georgiana. She confessed the plot to Darcy just in time for him to run Wickham off the property.

The letter does much to make Elizabeth reconsider her feelings toward Darcy. Back home, the militia is leaving town. Elizabeth turns cold toward Wickham, who turns his attentions to her more easily swayed younger sister, Lydia. Mr. Bennet reluctantly agrees to allow Lydia to spend the summer with friends in Brighton. This happens to be where Wickham's regiment will be stationed. During the summer, Elizabeth visits Pemberley, Darcy's large estate, in the company of Bennet relatives, the Gardiners. She enjoys the estate, thinking that Darcy is not there. Soon, however, Darcy appears. He is cordial to Elizabeth and the Gardiners and invites Elizabeth to meet his sister Georgiana.

Elizabeth soon receives a disturbing letter informing her that Lydia has run off with Wickham. Apparently, he promised her that they would run to Scotland where they could marry without her parents' permission, but instead he delayed the trip, risking ruining Lydia's reputation by living with her out of wedlock. Mr. Bennet and Mr. Gardiner head off to bring her back home, lest the situation cast a bad light on the entire family. The situation looks dire until the family receives a letter notifying them that Wickham has agreed to marry Lydia in exchange for an annual income. Mr. Bennet suspects that Mr. Gardiner provided the money, but Elizabeth learns later that it was, in fact, Mr. Darcy who saved her family's good name.

Lydia and Wickham arrive at the Bennets', where Mrs. Bennet is pleased to have at least one daughter now married. Mr. Bennet, however, is understandably cold toward the couple, and they leave to go north to Wickham's new assignment. Mr. Bingley returns to Netherfield and begins courting Jane again. He proposes, and all are pleased except his arrogant sister. As the family celebrates, they receive an unexpected visit from Lady Catherine de Bourgh. She confronts Elizabeth and insists that she knows that Darcy is about to propose to her and that she must promise her that she will refuse. She finds the prospect of marriage of a Darcy to a lower-class Bennet totally unacceptable. Elizabeth holds her ground and tells Lady Catherine that Darcy has not proposed, but that she will make no such promise setting limits on her future plans to anyone.

Not long afterward, Darcy and Elizabeth go for a walk during which Darcy tells her that he loves her as he always has and wishes to marry her. The novel ends happily with Jane and Elizabeth both getting married in successful matches.

Characters

Elizabeth Bennet is one of the most popular female protagonists in world literature. Readers admire her spirit, wit, intelligence, and strength of will. The victorious scene near the end of the novel where she stands up to Lady Catherine shows just how strong a character she is. She will not allow a woman's rank and power to force her to make promises against her own happiness.

Like all well-drawn characters in literature, however, Elizabeth is not without her faults. Like Mr. Darcy, she is proud of her heritage. She loves her father dearly and is proud that she comes from a gentleman's family. She is not overbearing in her pride to the point of arrogance, however. Another weakness is that she is quick to judge, especially when she hears something negative about someone. The example of misjudging Mr. Darcy based on Wickham's accusations nearly costs her happiness. Rather than confront Darcy or go about finding out more about the situation, she takes the easier way out and believes what she has heard, putting it alongside impressions she has formed of him based on little knowledge.

Mr. Darcy comes across to many readers as a complex character. He knows his place in society as the heir to his family estate. His discomfort at balls and other social gatherings may be the result of unease in social settings or other reasons. He tells Mr. Bingley, for example, that he does not like to dance. This must have made attending the social ritual of balls particularly unpleasant for him. As it is of shy people everywhere, it is easy to think of Darcy as arrogant only because he seems so

The BBC version of *Pride and Prejudice* features Colin Firth as the brooding Mr. Darcy (left) and Crispin Bonham-Carter as the easy-going Mr. Bingley.

aloof. Darcy is also guilty of making unfortunate comments when he is in a bad mood. When Bingley encourages him to dance with Elizabeth Bennet, for example, he tells Bingley that Bingley's partner is the only "handsome" woman in the room. When he lays eyes on Elizabeth for the first time at Bingley's pointing her out, he says grumpily, "She is tolerable; but not handsome enough to tempt me; and I am in no humour at present to give consequence to young ladies who are slighted by other men. You had better return to your partner and enjoy her smiles, for you are wasting your time with me."[2] Darcy has made a rather hasty judgment of Elizabeth. Elizabeth is taken aback at the slight, but rather than be offended, she is good-natured and high-spirited enough to find the whole thing rather funny; it is so obvious to her that Darcy feels out of place and out of sorts.

In short, both main characters of the novel show both pride and prejudice in their natures.

Techniques and Themes

Literary critic Mary Lascelles sees one of the chief techniques Austen employs in *Pride and Prejudice* as one of symmetry,

PRIDE AND PREJUDICE IN FILM

Nearly two hundred years after its initial publication, the story of *Pride and Prejudice* remains popular among readers and moviegoers. The 2005 film adaptation starring Keira Knightley as Elizabeth Bennet grossed over $38 million by early 2006. Though many Austen purists decried the liberties taken with the novel in the screenplay and disputed Knightley's performance, Knightley was nominated for an Academy Award for Best Actress for the role.

similar to that she initially used with the characters of *Sense and Sensibility*.[3] Here, however, she moves characters toward one another (principally Elizabeth Bennet and Darcy) by moving them apart at the same time. That is, neither really sees that much that is desirable in the other until they both are moved close enough to become nearly convinced of that undesirability. Austen has made the inherent flaws of her two principal characters obstacles to their finding happiness in each other. Darcy has become fairly tired of the Bennet family and its many daughters and the whole social scene they represent to him, while Elizabeth has found less and less in Darcy to like as she shifts her attention to Wickham, who seems, on the surface, to be the nicer person. When Bingley leaves and Wickham tells his lies to Elizabeth about why, she is all too prepared to accept his reasons as true.

Just as they are about to convince themselves of their respective judgments, however, a seed of doubt is planted in both Darcy and Elizabeth, or rather the seed that was planted early on begins to grow. Here, Austen uses other characters as further obstacles to Darcy's and Elizabeth's happiness. Lady Catherine seems resolute in seeing that they not be together. Elizabeth is surprised to be faced with her at her own home, where she is asked to promise never to marry Darcy. It becomes clear that Wickham does not want Darcy to be happy after the way Darcy foiled his plans with Georgiana. Once confronted with others' desires that they stay apart, the characters, who have been moving slowly back together, now depend solely on their own impressions of each other to make their final decision to marry.

protagonist

The main character of a story.

The novel was titled *First Impressions* clearly for a good reason. First impressions play a large part in the pride and prejudice that take place in the story. While Elizabeth and Darcy are both proud characters, neither is so full of pride that he or she truly abuses other people. They are both guilty of prejudging, however, most of all with each other. Their pride allows them to prejudge each other, but it is also the virtue that saves both of them from a very different future in the end. Elizabeth's pride in her family allows her to stand up to Lady Catherine while at the same time to be grateful to Darcy for what he has done for Lydia and her family. Darcy's pride in keeping his help to Lydia a secret and his intentions for

Keira Knightley (seated) stars as Elizabeth Bennett in the 2005 film version of *Pride and Prejudice*.

Elizabeth pure no matter what Lady Catherine's interference may be allow him to tell Elizabeth his true feelings not once, but twice.

In addition to the pride and prejudice themes mentioned in the title, another theme the novel addresses is the role of rank in marriage in early nineteenth-century Britain. At that place and time, one was expected not to marry outside one's rank and class. Mr. Darcy is expected to marry better than a gentleman's daughter. Austen suggests through this novel and her other works that love should rule in matters of the heart, not outside factors, such as rank or money. In her time, Austen's novel broke the mold in what it says and how it says it.

Austen seems to have been pleased with the publication of *Pride and Prejudice* in January 1813. She wrote to Cassandra about seeing the first copy of her "own darling Child"[4] arrive and about how they created a ruse under which to begin reading it that evening, even as a Miss Benn dined with them:

> Miss Benn dined with us on the very day of the Books coming, & in the even we set fairly at it & read half the 1st vol. to her—prefacing that having intelligence from Henry that such a work wd [would] soon appear we had desired him to send it whenever it came out—& I believe it passed with her unsuspected.—She was . . . amused, poor soul! *that* she [could] not help you know, with two such people to lead the way; but she really does seem to admire Elizabeth. I must confess that I think her as delightful a creature as ever appeared in print, & how I shall be able to tolerate those who do not like *her* at least, I do not know.[5]

She need not have been too concerned. The first review in *The British Critic* in February 1813 set the tone for the novel's future. "It is very far superior to almost all the publications of the kind which have lately come before us . . . the story is well told, the characters remarkably well drawn and supported, and written with great spirit as well as vigour."[6] Miss Milbanke, the future Lady Byron, commented:

> I have finished the Novel called *Pride and Prejudice*, which I think a very superior work. It depends not on any of the common resources of novel writers, no drownings, no conflagrations, nor runaway horses, nor lap-dogs and parrots, nor chambermaids and milliners, nor rencontres and disguises. I really think it is the most probable fiction I have ever read . . . I wish much to know who is the author or -ess as I am told—[7]

The early reviews of the book made it popular that season, and it sold well enough that a second printing was required later in the year. Readers from Austen's time until today have noted that *Pride and Prejudice* is overall a happy story. Austen herself, writing to Cassandra about printing and other errors she kept finding in her first pass through the volumes, writes that it may even be too light:

> The work is rather too light & bright & sparkling;—it wants shade;—it wants to be stretched out here & there with a long Chapter—of sense if it could be had, if not of solemn specious nonsense—about something unconnected with the story; an Essay on Writing, a critique on Walter Scott, or the history of Buonaparte—or anything that would form a contrast & bring the reader with increased delight to the playfulness & Epigrammatism of the general stile.[8]

Though most agree that the novel is "light" in the sense that it is entertaining, most critics also agree that it is not "light" as in not important. In his essay, "*Pride and Prejudice*:

The Limits of Society," James Sherry argues that while many readers see a theme of the individual versus society in *Pride and Prejudice*, they should be cautious about making the assumption that Austen writes too abstractly about Society. "[I]t is important . . . that the issues of *Pride and Prejudice* are much less abstract and much more localized than sometimes stated."[9] Marilyn Butler suggests that readers look beyond the common comparisons between Elizabeth and Darcy—she being more independent and less formal and he being more traditional and formal; her relatives as loving but less well-to-do; his relatives being wealthy but haughty. She points to a complexity of character on both of their parts, especially when considered alongside Jane Bennet and Charles Bingley and suggests that comparing the couples may be a more fruitful line of literary analysis.[10]

Whether read for entertainment as a "happy" novel, viewed in adaptation on the screen for the same reason, or studied more in depth for analysis, *Pride and Prejudice* seems destined to remain one of Austen's most revered works.

7 A Problematic Novel: *Mansfield Park*

Mansfield Park marks the first of what most scholars identify as Austen's mature novels. This designation is given to the three more complex novels that were begun, finished, and revised for publication all at Chawton Cottage (the other two being *Emma* and *Persuasion*). Interestingly, after *Mansfield Park*'s publication in 1814, Austen collected "reviews" of the book from family members and friends and recorded many of them in her letters. Her mother, for example, had "not liked it so well as *P. & P.*—Thought Fanny insipid.—Enjoyed Mrs. Norris." The author's sister Cassandra "thought it quite as clever, tho' not so brilliant, as *P. & P.*—Fond of Fanny—Delighted much in Mr. Rushworth's stupidity," while the families at Deane (a village in Hampshire) were "all pleased with it—Mrs. Anna Harwood delighted with Mrs. Norris & the green Curtain."[1]

Plot

Fanny Price is a young girl who moves in with her wealthy aunt and uncle, Sir Thomas and Lady Bertram, at their estate, Mansfield Park. Fanny comes from a poor family. Her mother, Lady Bertram's sister, married beneath her class, and her father, a sailor, drinks heavily and is disabled. At Mansfield Park, Fanny is not treated well by another aunt, busybody Mrs. Norris. Fanny's cousins treat her in different ways. Maria and Julia are arrogant and want only to marry rich. They see

Fanny as their poor relation who their family has taken in as a charity case. Tom, the older male cousin, is hinted about in his absence as being rowdy and drunk much of the time. Fanny finds solace predominantly in the younger male cousin, Edmund, who hopes to join the clergy and is kind to her.

Sir Thomas goes to Antigua to look after his plantations; this is one of the few slight references in Austen's novels to slavery and the wealth that is made from it in Britain. While Sir Thomas is away, the siblings of the local clergyman, Henry and Mary Crawford, arrive for an extended visit. Henry flirts with Edmund's sister, Maria, who is engaged to the wealthy but uninteresting Mr. Rushworth, but he also flirts with Julia on occasion. Mary Crawford first thinks she may be inter-

Cottesbrooke Hall in Northamptonshire is believed to have been the inspiration for the estate of Mansfield Park in Austen's novel.

ested in Tom Bertram, the heir to Mansfield Park, but she soon decides that he is boring and begins to be attracted to Edmund. However, marrying a clergyman is not a serious part of her plans. She begins to take this discomfort out on Edmund. Fanny, in the meantime, has fallen in love with Edmund herself.

Another visitor arrives on the scene—Yates, a friend of Tom Bertram's. He proposes that the group put on a play, *Lovers' Vows*, for their mutual entertainment. Neither Edmund nor Fanny wants to act. Edmund is pressed into it and ends up acting with Mary alongside Maria and Henry. The play is suggestive, and the actors become more and more infatuated with one another as they rehearse their parts. Fanny is nearly put upon to perform in the play as well, but before she does, Sir Thomas returns and puts an end to the inappropriate play-acting.

Since Henry does not make his love known to Maria, she marries Mr. Rushworth. She and Julia go to London. The relationship between Edmund and Mary continues its ups and downs with Edmund thinking he may propose. He is continually put off at the last minute, however, by Mary's lack of morality, her cruelty, and condescending attitude. He confides in Fanny about this, which upsets her, but Fanny keeps her feelings to herself. On a whim, Henry Crawford decides to court Fanny, but as he does so, he realizes that he has fallen in love with her.

Fanny has become a valuable part of the Mansfield Park family. When her brother William arrives, a ball is given in her honor. Afterward, Henry helps William get a promotion in the navy and uses this to try to influence Fanny's feelings for him. Fanny refuses Henry's proposal, and in retribution, her uncle temporarily sends her away from Mansfield Park, back to her home in poverty.

In the meantime, Edmund has been ordained and is still working out his feelings for Mary Crawford, to Fanny's distress. Henry follows Fanny to her poor home and tries to woo her there. Failing, he leaves, supposedly to go back to his own estate. Tom Bertram drinks too much and nearly dies from an accident. Henry is found out to have taken Maria from her husband and run away with her. Julia is so upset by this that she marries Tom's friend, Yates. Edmund finally experiences the last straw with Mary when she admits that she would not mind seeing Tom die so that Edmund could become the heir to Mansfield Park. Fanny is invited back to the Bertram estate, and with her she brings her sister, Susan.

The story ends with Maria breaking up with Henry to go live with Mrs. Norris on the European continent. Maria and Henry, along with Mary, are cast out of the graces of Mansfield Park. Fanny consoles Edmund for his loss with Mary, but he finally sees that Fanny has been the woman for him all along. He and Fanny marry, and Susan continues to live on well with the Bertrams, taking on Fanny's former role.

Characters

Fanny Price seems to be a divisive character for readers of Jane Austen. She is the only major character in Austen's fiction who is depicted as a child (when she first moves to Mansfield Park), and some evidence suggests that Austen was especially fond of her.[2] Readers either like Fanny in large measure or dislike her to the same degree. Author Lionel Trilling was among the latter. He wrote: "Nobody, I believe, has ever found it possible to like the heroine of *Mansfield Park*."[3] Twentieth-century British writer C. S. Lewis found Fanny Price too passive

Austen and the Three Sisters

Mansfield Park, and especially its opening describing the three Ward sisters (Fanny's aunts), has brought to the attention of some readers that Austen frequently includes a trio of sisters in her works. The three sisters in this novel are Maria Ward (Lady Bertram), who married wealthy Sir Thomas; Mrs. Norris, who married the Reverend Mr. Norris; and Frances Ward, Fanny's mother, who married Lieutenant Price who had no "education, fortune, or connections."[4] Fanny becomes a de facto third sister of the Bertram girls, Maria and Julia, when she lives at Mansfield Park, as well as being the actual third sister in her own family that includes Susan and Betsey.

In *Sense and Sensibility*, the three sisters are Marianne, Elinor, and Margaret Dashwood. In *Pride and Prejudice*, the main focus is on three of the five Bennet daughters—Jane, Elizabeth, and Lydia—and in *Persuasion*, there are three sisters: Anne, Elizabeth, and Mary Elliot.[5] The three sisters, of course, do not mimic Austen's own experience, since in her family there was just herself and her one sister, Cassandra.

and meek.[6] Citing these authors and others, including Nina Auerbach who likens Fanny to Dr. Frankenstein's monster, critic Amy J. Pawl writes: "*Mansfield Park* is a 'problem novel' because Fanny Price is a problem heroine."[7]

To some, Fanny represents absolute morality in that she believes in rather black-and-white definitions of right and wrong. She understands her place in society and in the Bertram family and does not attempt to cross boundaries. Some readers admire this and others see her as too prim and passive. While she seems to hold back at times when the reader might like to see her be more assertive, Fanny is not without backbone. She refuses to take part in the play *Lovers' Vows*, which she finds inappropriate. In addition, Fanny's clear understanding of propriety allows her to reason from what she has learned from Edmund and the good life she has been given at the Bertrams that she should not feel obligated to accept the proposal of a man she does not love.

The opposite of Fanny Price in the novel is the character Mary Crawford. Unlike Fanny, Mary is not attentive or sensitive to others. She can be cruel. She desires wealth even at the expense of love. She is beautiful and can be charming, but she has not been brought up well by her aunt and uncle, and she has been too influenced by her fashionable friends. She is often called amoral, since she appears willing to do or say almost anything to get what she wants.

Edmund Bertram is the character most like Fanny Price. Since he is the youngest son, he is not expected to take over Mansfield Park as the heir. Instead, he must find his own way in the world. Like Fanny, he accepts his position and attempts to make the best of it. He is sensitive to others, particularly Fanny, and her place in his family, even at an early age. Unlike Fanny, however, Edmund is taken in by the charms of someone who is not good for him when he becomes infatuated with Mary Crawford.

Techniques and Themes

Mansfield Park is Austen's first and only novel that uses omniscient third-person point of view to the degree that it does. In other words, the narrator of this novel, unlike in the others, depicts scenes in which the heroine is not present, and it addresses the consciousness of characters outside of the main

This late-nineteenth-century drawing depicts Fanny and Edmund in conversation in a scene from *Mansfield Park*.

A FELINE MRS. NORRIS

The author of the Harry Potter novels, J. K. Rowling, has admitted in interviews that she named the cat of Hogwarts' caretaker, Argus Filch, Mrs. Norris, after the busybody Mrs. Norris in *Mansfield Park*. Rowling said, "I'm big on names. I like names, generally . . . I also collect them from all sorts of places . . . Mrs. Norris, people will recognize, comes from Jane Austen."[8]

character.[9] This maneuvering allows for a psychological study of the characters in their various dynamics in the group.

This point of view allows the reader to understand more fully how different Mary is, for example, from Fanny, since the reader sees her when Fanny does not. Since the reader's eye can take in more than one character alone, the omniscient point of view enhances the novel's exploration of how environment affects personality.

This novel, perhaps even to a greater degree than the others, depicts the inside world of the wealthy. Fanny moves between the two worlds of poverty and wealth, and she does not ignore the fact that her surroundings in each place speak volumes about the differences. Critic John Wiltshire points out the importance of property in this novel. He argues that here Austen accomplishes a first in the British novel—the placement of her characters within certain settings with full knowledge of the settings' relevance to the characters and their futures. "The novelist imagines the physical world in which her figures move to have a palpable presence, an effective bearing on their lives . . . Characters and their bodies are imagined precisely within settings that are drawn into the narrative and act as provocations to conversation and action."[10] In other words, in this novel in particular, Austen illustrates how setting affects the way characters behave and the way they develop.

The novel is frequently said to have at least two prominent themes. One theme has to do with morality, especially the concept of absolute morality versus situational ethics. The other theme concerns the role of property and social class on the development of character.

Austen must have been particularly curious about what people would think of her new novel, since it was the first she had started and completed in over a decade. Reviews of *Mansfield Park* were positive when the book came out. Many reviews applauded the then unknown author of *Sense and Sensibility* and *Pride and Prejudice*'s theme of absolute morality versus situational ethics. Absolute morality prescribes that there is a right and wrong way to do things, and situations should not change one's behavior in regard to moral issues. In contrast, situational ethics dictates that one should examine each individual situation for what is the right thing to do and that different situations may require different responses. Fanny may be said to represent absolute morality, and her cousins Maria and Julia, as well as Mary Crawford, may represent situational ethics. Austen seems to favor absolute morality that guides a life over time to situational ethics that are subject to change according to the specific circumstances.

omniscient point of view

A "godlike" narrator that tells the story and can tell what characters are thinking.

The novel also addresses the theme of social class and its effect on character. Most of the characters who have had the advantages of a secure, clean, and elaborate home take it for granted and do not feel compassionate toward those who do not have such an environment. Many of the characters who have made it, through marriage or inheritance, to such a wealthy home tend to forget where they came from and look down their noses at those who are less fortunate. The more favorable characters in Austen's novels look at people for their own worth as human beings, regardless of their social standing in society.

Readers at the time must have noticed Austen's critique of the upper and upwardly mobile social class in this novel.

Fanny (Frances O'Connor) and Henry Crawford (Alessandro Nivola) dance in a scene from the 1999 film version of *Mansfield Park*.

Unlike her more lighthearted criticisms in her previous work, *Mansfield Park* takes on the theme more directly. Mary Lascelles notes that Austen must have known she had created a new work at a different level after she finished writing this first mature work so many years after her last completed novel. "She must have known that *Mansfield Park* excelled *Pride and Prejudice* in its subtler conception of human relations—by as much *Pride and Prejudice* had excelled *Sense and Sensibility* in its more subtly planned construction."[11]

8 "Perfect" *Emma*

Austen's fifth novel, the fourth one to be published, begins this way: "Emma Woodhouse, handsome, clever, and rich, with a comfortable home and happy disposition, seemed to unite some of the best blessings of existence; and had lived nearly twenty-one years in the world with very little to distress or vex her."[1]

This first sentence would become another of the most famous first lines in world literature. Appearing in December 1815, *Emma* has been regarded by literary critics and scholars as Austen's "perfect novel." In Austen's own time, writer Sir Walter Scott wrote an influential review of *Emma*, as Paul Poplawski describes, "praising it for its verisimilitude, its narrative control, and its precision of language and characterization, [he] saw it as an important new departure for fiction toward greater realism."[2] Scott's words about Austen's realism were, "copying from nature as she [nature] really exists in the common walks of life, and presenting to the reader, instead of the splendid scenes of an imaginary world, a correct and striking representation of that which is daily taking place around him."[3] Poplawski relates that *Emma* is still regarded highly among critics and writers today. It is often regarded as "one of the first (if not *the* first) fully achieved modern novels, as well as one of the best."[4]

Plot

Emma Woodhouse is twenty years old and lives with her father. Her mother died some time ago, and she has no siblings remaining at home. Unlike many women her age at that time, Emma is not that interested in marrying. Instead, she finds entertainment value in making matches for others. As the novel opens, she has just done so successfully by matching up her governess and Mr. Weston, a widower from the village. Despite her satisfaction with the match, Emma grows lonely after the governess leaves the house. Soon, though, she has a new friend, Harriet Smith. She wants to bring Harriet, who does not know her parentage, up in social class by educating her and helping her to marry well. She frowns on the kind farmer, Robert Martin, who genuinely seems to care for Harriet. Instead, she encourages Harriet to admire Mr. Elton, the village vicar, who is of higher standing.

There is one problem from the start with Emma's new matchmaking scheme, and that is that Mr. Elton prefers her to Harriet. Emma's brother-in-law (brother to her sister's husband), Mr. Knightley, frequently visits Emma and her father. He watches Emma's plotting with amusement but warns her that Robert Martin really is a good match for Harriet Smith. Mr. Elton responds to his rejection by Emma and his offense at her suggestion that Harriet is good enough for him by leaving, going to Bath, and marrying someone there nearly at once.

SIR WALTER SCOTT

Sir Walter Scott (1771–1832) was a Scottish novelist and poet. Some critics consider him the originator of the regional novel and the historical novel. As such, he was one of the most influential novelists of the early nineteenth century. The title he is most known for today is his historical novel, *Ivanhoe* (1820).[5]

Novelist, playwright, and poet Sir Walter Scott wrote a review of *Emma* upon its publication, praising its realism.

Two newer visitors to Highbury attract Emma's attention—Jane Fairfax, who seems too reserved for Emma to get close to, and the enthusiastic Frank Churchill, Mr. Weston's son, who arrives on the scene eager to socialize. Emma thinks Mr. Churchill may be interested in her and readily flirts with him. Churchill raises the suspicions of Mr. Knightley, however, especially when Churchill rides horseback all the way to London and back, simply to get his hair cut. Meanwhile, Knightley defends Jane Fairfax to Emma, pointing out that, unlike Emma who may enjoy the living quarters she has had with her father and her family for as long as she likes, Jane is doomed to become a governess very soon.

Eventually, Emma begins thinking of a new match between Harriet and Frank Churchill. When Harriet is embarrassed by Mr. Elton and his wife, Mr. Knightley attracts Emma's attention in a new way by rescuing Harriet in asking her to dance. Harriet is then saved from a mugging by Gypsies the next day by Frank. When she tells Emma that she has fallen in love with someone above her in social class, Emma thinks this must be Frank. However, Harriet has taken a liking to Mr. Knightley.

It turns out that there is a secret in the plot of *Emma*. Frank Churchill did not come to visit his father after so many years to foster their relationship. In fact, he has been secretly engaged to Jane Fairfax and came to Highbury to be near her. His attention to Emma has been a ruse to keep others from finding out. Mr. Knightley tries to warn Emma of an attachment between Frank and Jane at a picnic, but Emma ends up offending kindly Miss Bates. Mr. Knightley, who knows Emma's faults as well as her strengths, helps her see this, and she feels upset for what she did.

When Frank's aunt dies, his uncle approves of his match, and he is free to marry Jane. When Harriet confesses to Emma

OTHER FAMOUS BRITISH EMMAS

The name "Emma" was popular in Jane Austen's day and it has enjoyed a great deal of popularity in recent years as well. Some famous British Emmas can even claim a link to Austen. Emma Thompson is an Academy Award-winning actor, who has adapted at least one Jane Austen novel into a screenplay. Emma Watson is the actor who played Hermione Granger in the popular Harry Potter films. Perhaps J. K. Rowling, the British author of the famous Harry Potter series, particularly enjoyed the casting of Emma Watson. She has said in interviews that Jane Austen's *Emma* is her favorite novel.

the identity of her love interest, Mr. Knightley, Emma realizes that she has fallen in love with him herself. She thinks Knightley must also love Harriet, but instead he tells her that it is she whom he loves. Jilted a second time, Harriet is upset until, conveniently, Robert Martin proposes to her again, and she accepts. This allows Mr. Knightley and Emma to marry with clear consciences as well.

Characters

Many of today's readers especially like Emma Woodhouse among Austen's characters. She is the only main female character in Austen's fiction who does not need to marry to have a place to live, and she does not have marriage on her mind at the beginning of the story. This is in keeping with her character, but it is also a fact of her place on the social ladder. She is free to live with her father for as long as she needs.

In addition, Emma's relationship with Mr. Knightley develops over many years. She is independent and spirited, though, of course, flawed in that she thinks enough of herself that she can affect the future of others by being in charge of their love matches. Instead of focusing on pairs of characters as she does in *Sense and Sensibility* and *Pride and Prejudice*, in *Emma* Austen directs the readers' attentions primarily to the title character. The novel may be said to be about the education and development of one woman: Emma Woodhouse.

Unlike Mr. Woodhouse, who is too concerned about everyone's health to see much beyond that, or Harriet Smith, who respects Emma as a young woman who is eager to help her advance, Mr. Knightley is perhaps the only character to see Emma's faults. He mentions them frequently throughout

Gwyneth Paltrow plays the title role in the 1996 film *Emma*.

A ROYAL DEDICATION

Having already published *Sense and Sensibility*, *Pride and Prejudice*, and *Mansfield Park*, Austen had a fan in the Prince Regent by the time *Emma* was to be published. James Stanier Clarke, writing from Carlton House, November 16, 1815, informed her, "It is certainly not incumbent on you to dedicate your work now in the Press to His Royal Highness: but if you wish to do the Regent that honour either now or at any future period, I am happy to send you that permission which need not require any more trouble or solicitation on your Part."[6]

At first Austen did not think she would do this. She had a rather less than favorable view of the flamboyant Prince Regent and, in particular, his well-known womanizing. However, she was later told that a suggestion from the Prince Regent that she had the permission to honor him was really a command, so she obliged. Her dedication, as sent in a letter to her publisher, was fairly straightforward: "The Title page must be, Emma, Dedicated by Permission to H. R. H. The Prince Regent."[7] The actual, more extravagant dedication with its three "Royal Highnesses," was most likely inserted by the publisher. It reads:

To
His Royal Highness
THE PRINCE REGENT,
This work is,
By His Royal Highness's Permission,
Most Respectfully
Dedicated,
By His Royal Highness's
Dutiful
And Obedient
Humble Servant,
THE AUTHOR.[8]

the story, and it is he who sees her matchmaking for what it is. Readers have the sense that, since he has known her since she was a child, when her sister married his brother, he knows her from a loving but also fair and objective perspective. Austen has designed Emma as a character such that readers see how right Mr. Knightley is for her. She is too intelligent and self-possessed to be taken in by someone who does not know her bad side as well as her good side.

Techniques and Themes

By focusing the narrative on the title character, Austen is able to explore in more depth her territory of relationships among a few country families. She has moved beyond the pairing of sisters of the earlier novels that still echo with the shadows of their former epistolary forms. She has limited the point of view more closely to her main character, more so than in her omniscient point of view depicting Fanny Price in *Mansfield Park*. Even though events happen to Harriet Smith and others in this novel, the book is clearly Emma's story.

Through following Emma's development, the reader may interpret a theme about one's self-worth. Certainly, matchmaking is an obvious subject, and Emma comes across as both successful and unsuccessful in her efforts at matching up other people. She also comes across, however, as thinking a bit too highly of herself. Matchmaking is something she believes she has a talent for with apparently no regard for how much her interference intrudes on other people's lives. As much as the reader may like Emma, the character can be seen as slightly dangerous in that she attempts to step out of the marriage game herself in order to be in a position of control over it in the lives of other people.

A Modern Take on *Emma*

In a departure from the many period pieces adapting Austen's novels for the cinema, the 1995 film *Clueless* is inspired by *Emma* but set in contemporary times. The Emma-like character, Cher, played by Alicia Silverstone, is a rich teenager from Beverly Hills who plays matchmaker for two of her teachers. Afterward, Cher and her rich friend, Dionne, decide to do a "makeover" on a new transfer student, Tai. Through the process, however, Cher grows beyond superficial concerns into a young woman who cares about the depth of character in herself and others. The film was written and directed by Amy Heckerling.

In Austen's time, marrying above one's station was frowned upon. To "marry up or down" threw off the social order. Austen appears unafraid to reveal the follies of this convention in her work. In this novel, however, although Emma tries to help Harriet Smith rise above her expected station in life, Harriet still ends up marrying well, but within her social and economic rank. If Harriet were to "marry up," whether for love or for wealth, one interpretation of the story might be that this is something she should accomplish herself, not through the meddling or manipulation of someone else, even someone with good intentions.

Mr. Knightley, as a character representing ethical behavior and common sense, perhaps enjoys watching the marriage game happening around him as much as Emma does, but he does not participate in it or interfere with the lives of others, except when he might help keep someone from harm, as in "rescuing" Harriet Smith from humiliation when he asks her to dance. Because he knows his place is to observe but not

The 1998 film *Clueless* starring Alicia Silverstone is a modern retelling of *Emma*. The film is considered a cult classic.

meddle in the affairs of others, he is seen by many readers as mature and wise.

When he and Emma find their way to each other at the end of the novel, there is a revelation of recognition, not of discovery. As John Wiltshire observes, "What Emma learns in this novel is not to think like Mr. Knightley, but that she has always, in fact, thought like him. There is no element of capitulation in the novel's ending, rather one of celebratory recognition."[9]

This is another reason why some feminists and more recent scholars and critics praise *Emma* highly among Austen's novels. Emma has looked for occupation in her matchmaking, but she is not doing it for evil or selfish purposes as some of the women in Austen's other novels do. She operates primarily from a secure and wise place. However, throughout the novel she matures to realize that her innocent actions are interferences, nonetheless. Other feminist readers disagree with this characterization of Emma as strong and independent. They argue the reverse of John Wiltshire's point by claiming that, in the end, Emma yields to Mr. Knightley's patriarchal authority.

9 Juvenilia and Posthumous Works

Rounding out Austen's novels are two more that were published after her death by her brother, Henry. In addition to *Sense and Sensibility*, *Pride and Prejudice*, *Mansfield Park*, and *Emma*, all of which were published in her lifetime, Austen's major works include *Northanger Abbey* and *Persuasion*. Besides these posthumous works, Austen scholars are also interested in studying her many writings as a teenager and developing writer.

Juvenilia

In tracing authors' developments as artists, scholars often find their earlier writing illuminating. Jane Austen does not disappoint scholars searching for evidence of her earlier writing, since so much of her juvenilia survives. In fact, Austen herself preserved her early writing in three volumes she labeled Volume I, Volume II, and Volume III. The notebooks contain poems, stories, a novel in letters called *Love and Freindship* (Austen's spelling), short writing sketches, and several other kinds of playful and experimental works.

History of England

Perhaps one of the most well known of Jane Austen's writing efforts as a young person is her *History of England*. Austen wrote her little book when she was not quite sixteen years old. It is a parody of Oliver Goldsmith's four-volume *History of*

England that was in her father's library and which virtually all students read at the time. What intrigues many scholars about Austen's *History* is its comic irony that would become one of her signatures styles years later in her novels. As A. S. Byatt says in her introduction to the facsimile edition published by Algonquin Books, "The *History of England* is poking fun at matter-of-fact abridgments of history, in which deaths and disasters are reduced to educational *facts* to be digested. It is somewhere between deadpan farce in tone, and a kind of wild early irony."[1]

The history contains thirteen chapters: "Henry the 4th," "Henry the 5th," "Henry the 6th," "Edward the 4th," "Edward the 5th," "Richard the 3rd," "Henry the 7th," "Henry the 8th,"

Austen's childhood years in the village of Steventon, pictured here, were happy and productive. Her early writings reveal hints of the novelist she would one day become.

"Edward the 6th," "Mary," "Elizabeth," "James the 1st," and "Charles the 1st." Cassandra Austen drew the sometimes less than regal depictions of each figure. The manuscript is dated Saturday, November 16, 1791. The book pokes fun at the narrators of history more than it does at the figures written about as this passage from "Henry the 6th" illustrates:

irony

Figure of speech that says one thing but means another. In comic irony, this disconnect creates a humorous, sarcastic, or mocking effect.

facsimile

A photographic image of a document, book, or other material, frequently published in book form.

> I suppose you know all about the Wars between him and the Duke of York who was of the right side; If you do not, you had better read some other History, for I shall not be very diffuse in this, meaning by it only to vent my Spleen *against*, & shew my Hatred *to* all those people whose parties or principles do not suit with mine, & not to give information.[2]

Austen collected the juvenilia in the three surviving volumes but did not put them away for safekeeping and never looked at them again. There is evidence that the volumes were opened and turned to several times over the years. She may have shown them to nieces and nephews who were also interested in writing, since her letters give this kind of advice to young relatives. Pieces in each volume are: Volume I: *Frederic and Elfrida* ("a novel"); *Jack and Alice* ("a novel"); *Edgar and Emma* ("a tale"); *Henry and Eliza* ("a novel"); *The adventures of Mr. Harley* ("a short, but interesting Tale"); *Sir William Mountague* ("an unfinished performance"); *Memoirs of Mr. Clifford* ("an unfinished tale"); *The Beautifull Cassandra* ("a novel in twelve Chapters"); *Amelia Webster* ("a tale in letters"); *The Visit* ("a comedy in two acts"); *The Mystery* ("an unfinished comedy"); *The Three Sisters* ("a novel"); and separate pieces, "A beautiful description of the different effects of Sensibility on different Minds"; "The generous Curate"; and "Ode to Pity."

Volume II contains *Love and Freindship* ("a novel in a series of letters"—and spelled that way); *Lesley Castle* ("an unfinished novel in letters"); *The History of England*; *A Collection of Letters*; and scraps that include a letter to Miss Fanny Catherine Austen; "The female philosopher" ("a letter"); "The first Act of a Comedy"; "A Letter from a Young Lady"; "A Tour through Wales—in a Letter from a Young Lady—"; and "A Tale." *Love and Freindship*, a sustained work written when Austen was about fifteen years old, pokes fun at the "sentimental" heroines of the romance novels of her day and their overly emotional responses to events.

Finally, in Volume III there are: "Evelyn" and "Catharine, or the Bower." Other writings not contained in the three notebooks include the "Plan of a Novel, according to hints from various quarters" and several verses and prayers.[3] A sampling of one of her verses shows Austen's humor developing at an early age. Each line rhymes with the word "rose":

Happy the lab'rer [laborer] in his Sunday clothes!
In light-drab coat, smart waistcoat, well-darn'd hose,
And hat upon his head, to church he goes;
As oft, with conscious pride, he downward throws
A glance upon the ample cabbage rose
That, stuck in button-hole, regales his nose,
He envies not the gayest London beaux.
In church he takes his seat among the rows,
Pays to the pace the reverence he owes,

Likes best the prayers whose meaning least he knows,
Lists to the sermon in a softening doze,
And rouses joyous at the welcome close.[4]

Northanger Abbey

After Austen's death in 1817, her brother Henry saw to it that two of her remaining novel manuscripts were published by John Murray. They were *Northanger Abbey* and *Persuasion*, which came out very late in the year of the author's death. *Northanger Abbey* was actually the first book Austen sold to a publisher. Her sister, Cassandra, claimed that she wrote the novel in 1798 and 1799 and sold it to Crosby and Co. in 1803 under the different title of *Susan*. The publisher held on to the manuscript but did not publish it. Advertisements publicized the novel, yet still it did not appear

JANE AUSTEN'S HUMOROUS *HISTORY OF ENGLAND*

The title page of Austen's *History* shows its comic intent and use of irony:

The History of
England
From the Reign of
Henry the 4th
To the Death of
Charles the 1st
By a partial, prejudiced, & ignorant Historian
To Miss Austen, eldest daughter of the Revd. George Austen,
This Work is inscribed with all due respect by
The Author
N. B. There will be very few Dates in this History.

On April 5, 1809, Austen wrote to Crosby and Co. demanding that the book either be published immediately or be released to her to publish elsewhere. She signed the letter with a pseudonym, "Mrs. Ashton Dennis," that allowed her to initial the letter, "M.A.D."[5] Crosby and Co. threatened her with legal action. Finally, in 1816, Henry Austen purchased the manuscript back from the publisher for the price they had paid for it. Crosby and Co. was not aware that Henry was purchasing a manuscript that was written by the anonymous author of the successful *Pride and Prejudice* and *Sense and Sensibility*. Austen was helped greatly by her brother in terms of publication of all of her work. However, the persistence and attention to the business side of publication that she possessed as a professional woman writer, proven in her letters, has often been underestimated.[6]

Northanger Abbey is chiefly regarded by Austen scholars as a novel about novels and writing. Unlike her other books, this one does not seamlessly immerse the reader into the "reality" of a fictional world, and it does not have characters that are developed to the point that readers believe they could recognize them on the street, as many Austen readers say they could do. Instead, this novel opens with a discussion of Catherine Morland as a heroine figure, even though she is very ordinary and would not strike most readers as a prospect for a heroine in a novel. Austen keeps the reader's attention focused on the question of Catherine Morland as a heroine in a novel rather than accepting automatically that she is the heroine and moving on with the story. This kind of fiction that questions itself and its own creation within the story is called metafiction.

The book is made up of two books and is about the coming-of-age of Catherine Morland, who goes to Bath for the

Heroine Catherine Morland, an avid reader of gothic novels, allows her imagination to run wild in *Northanger Abbey*.

Metafiction

Metafiction is a kind of fiction that is self-conscious about its own techniques. It contains references within the story or novel to how stories and novels are written and/or read. A classic example of a twentieth-century work of metafiction is John Barth's collection of short stories, *Lost in the Funhouse* (1968). Metafiction may draw attention to the creation of fiction in many ways. For example, the characters may be aware that they are in a work of fiction; the author may break the flow of the story to comment on the characters or the action or the writing; a story may contain references to its own title, plot, setting, or other elements; and so forth.

season where she is the guest of Mr. and Mrs. Allen. While she is there, she meets an eccentric character, General Tilney, and his son and daughter, Henry and Elanor. Catherine is invited to the Tilney home, which is the Northanger Abbey of the title. At Northanger Abbey, her reading of gothic romances and other popular fiction of Jane Austen's youth works on her imagination until she begins to envision secrets lurking about the place. Henry proves to her that these imaginings are not true, and Catherine is humiliated. General Tilney orders her to leave Northanger Abbey. Henry follows her home and explains to her that his father sought to protect him from her, thinking she had no money. All is well when the general is told the truth and gives his blessing to Henry to marry Catherine.

Most importantly, this shortest of Austen's major works makes fun of gothic novels, most notably those of the popular novelist of her youth, Ann Radcliffe. It may represent, in fictional form, Austen's own theories about the literary art form of the novel as she was working in it and as she would later help to change it. Ironically, Catherine Morland turns away from the gothic novel herself to accept a more realistic view of the world, just as Austen does in her writing.

Northanger Abbey was originally written before *Sense and Sensibility* and *Pride and Prejudice*, so it is not considered an example of Austen's mature work. It was also not revised as extensively as the other novels because she was working on the revisions in the final months of her life, when she was often ill. Despite this, many critics remain enthusiastic about the novel.

Persuasion

Published together with *Northanger Abbey* by Austen's brother Henry, *Persuasion* was titled by him after his sister's death. The novel is about Anne Elliott, Austen's eldest heroine at age twenty-eight. She is the daughter of Sir Walter Elliot, whose wife died fourteen years before. The Elliot family is of the landed gentry class. Anne has two sisters: Mary, who is married to wealthy Charles Musgrove and lives nearby, and Elizabeth, who is not married. At age twenty, Anne was persuaded by a family friend, Lady Russell, to reject her then suitor, Frederick Wentworth. Anne loved Frederick and Frederick loved her, but Lady Russell insisted he was not wealthy enough for a member of the Elliot family to marry.

Sir Walter spends too much money. Mortified, he and his daughters must go to Bath where they can live less expensively. Persuading Sir Walter that this is necessary is one of the first "persuasions" that takes place in the novel. They rent out their family estate, Kellynch Hall, to Admiral and Mrs. Croft. Mrs. Croft is Frederick Wentworth's sister. Rather than go to Bath with Sir Walter and Elizabeth right away, Anne stays nearby to help her sister Mary. There, she learns that Captain Wentworth has returned to his sister's at Kellynch Hall. When Anne sees him, however, he seems indifferent toward her now and seems more interested in Mary's sisters-in-law, Louisa and Henrietta.

This circle of family and friends arranges for a trip to Lyme. Friends of Frederick's live there—Captain Harville and his family as well as Captain Benwick, who is mourning the death of his fiancée, Harville's sister, Fanny. While there, Louisa Musgrove has an accident, and Frederick feels somewhat responsible. He becomes frustrated when it begins to appear that he may be expected to marry Louisa at the time he is beginning to think he may have a chance with Anne Elliot again after all. In the meantime, Anne goes to Bath where she meets William Elliot, Sir William's heir, who seems intent on marrying her.

The story resolves with Captain Benwick falling in love with Louisa Musgrove and Charles Hayter asking for the hand of Henrietta. This leaves Frederick available, which he is happy to be after overhearing Anne talking with Captain Harville about women's affections lasting forever. Since he is now also wealthier from his trip to sea, Sir Walter takes them into his social circle. There are no restrictions placed on the couple, and Frederick proposes to Anne. She accepts, and they are both happy.

One of the themes in the novel is definitely that of persuasion. Not only is Sir Walter persuaded to go to Bath, but Captain Wentworth is persuaded to visit the Mugroves; Henrietta is persuaded to accept the marriage offer from Charles Hayter. Anne persuades Captain Benwick to talk about his feelings for his lost love, Fanny Harville. William Elliot persuades Sir Walter to accept him after their family estrangement, and Louisa is persuaded to marry Captain Benwick. Anne and Captain Wentworth need to persuade

Looking on her with a face as pallid as her own.

An early illustration depicts the aftermath of Louisa Musgrove's fall, a dramatic scene and turning point in *Persuasion*.

themselves that each one still has feelings for the other these long years later.

The novel also addresses the theme of social class and money directly. That is, it explores the question of old money received through inheritance (demonstrated through Sir Walter and Elizabeth Elliot, etc.) versus new money received by those who have worked to earn it, such as the navy admirals. Austen seems to be saying that her society's placing higher value on inherited wealth should change and is changing at her time in favor of the rise of the middle class through hard work. Having three brothers in the navy no doubt sensitized Austen to the important role that individuals could play in the future of the country. Although inherited property and the resulting passivity on the part of characters play a big part in much of Austen's fiction, in *Persuasion*, characters take more of an active role in the outcome of their own destinies.

Jane Austen's juvenilia and the novels *Northanger Abbey* and *Persuasion*, the first two representing her earlier work and the latter one her later work, serve as bookends to her four other major novels.

Other Minor Austen Works

In addition to her juvenilia that scholars study for Austen's development as a writer, they also look at the unpublished novels or novel fragments for this purpose as well as to speculate on where her writing may have been heading, had she lived. *Lady Susan* was most likely written before 1805 but was not published until 1871 when it appeared as part of James Edward Austen-Leigh's *Memoir*. It is frequently cited as containing Austen's most "wicked" heroine. *The Watsons* was written between 1803 and 1805 and was probably set aside at the time of Mr. Austen's death. It also appeared in 1871 as part of the *Memoir*. It concerns the Watson sisters who live in a provincial town. Finally, there is an unfinished novel, *Sanditon*, written in Austen's later years but not published until 1925. That story was set in a seaside town and foreshadowed some of the coming social conflicts caused by the industrial revolution.[7]

Despite having published just four full novels in her lifetime, Jane Austen's legacy has persisted—and continues to grow—for over two centuries.

10 Austen's Legacy

Like great authors before and after her, the figure of Jane Austen has become as much a part of the legacy of world literature as her works. Her own story has been added to those of her novels as a subject of interest, interpretation, and debate among readers. In addition, even so many years later, Austen has become something nearing a "brand," to use today's vernacular. Her image, quotes from her novels, and other "Austenilia" appear in popular culture, in "Austenesque" works of fiction claiming to be inspired by her work, in social media, and in other places. The limits of where Austen's influence or references may appear seem to be expanding, rather than diminishing, with time.

Last Days

Sometime in the spring of 1816, Jane Austen began to feel ill. Later that year she suffered from back pain and other ailments but continued working as much as she could on her writing. She was now forty years old and could have attributed her aches and pains to age as many people did at the time, but hypochondria was not in her nature. She continued work on her novels, *Persuasion* (with the working title of *The Elliotts*) and *Northanger Abbey* (working title, *Susan*). Despite her work on these projects, there is only one surviving letter from the last three months of that year, which suggests that writing was not an activity that was easy for her to do during this period.[1]

In early 1817, she appeared to feel better. She was out of bed and walking into town, though she was too weak to walk back home. She wrote to one correspondent that she was suffering from "Bile," but that she had learned how to control it. To another she wrote that she had rheumatism, with pain in her knee only occasionally. By March, however, she was overtaken by high fever, and by mid-April she was spending her days in bed. On April 27, 1817, Jane Austen wrote out her last will and testament, giving everything she had to her sister, Cassandra.

In May, she accepted her family's decision to move her to Winchester for medical treatment. Her brothers Henry and William rode on horseback beside the carriage carrying Jane and Cassandra for all of the sixteen miles from Chawton. She and her sister stayed at No. 8 College Street. Her doctor administered treatment, and Jane received some temporary relief. However, she was not getting well.

In a letter, Cassandra described her sister's final hours. Cassandra had been by Jane's bedside unceasingly except for short breaks. Jane suffered a seizure, then calmed down, apparently unconscious. Some hours later, she roused again, able to talk with her sister enough to give her an account of the seizure. "God grant me patience," she said. "Pray for me. Oh Pray for me."[2] The doctor gave her some medication for pain. The author did not stir, and this made Cassandra believe that, though Jane knew she was dying, she was no longer suffering. Cassandra held Jane's head on her pillow. She writes of her dear younger sister, "in about one hour more she breathed her last. I was able to close her eyes myself & it was a great gratification to me to render her these last services."[3] Jane Austen's funeral took place on July 24, 1817, and she was buried in Winchester Cathedral.

Winchester Cathedral

Jane Austen was buried and memorialized at Winchester Cathedral in Hampshire. Her tombstone reads:

> In Memory of
> JANE AUSTEN,
> youngest daughter of the late
> Rev. GEORGE AUSTEN,
> formerly Rector of Steventon in this County
> she departed this Life on the 18th of July 1817
> aged 41, after a long illness supported with
> the patience and the hopes of a Christian.
> The benevolence of her heart,
> the sweetness of her temper, and
> the extraordinary endowments of her mind
> obtained the regard of all who knew her; and
> the warmest love of her intimate connections.
> Their grief is in proportion to their affection
> they know their loss to be irreparable,
> but in their deepest affliction they are consoled
> by a firm though humble hope that her charity
> devotion, faith and purity have rendered
> her soul acceptable in the sight of her
> REDEEMER.[4]

Interestingly, there is no mention at all on her tombstone of the titles of her works or even that she was a published author.

The Mystique of Jane Austen

Once Jane Austen died, almost immediately the telling of her life by those who cared about its perception by others began. Her reputation as a spinster and a retiring, devout, and humble woman who never married nor had many outward cares of her own began to appear in early accounts written by family members. They wanted to present her life to the public in what they thought was the most favorable light. For instance, in his "Biographical Notice of the Author" that accompanied the publication of *Northanger Abbey* and *Persuasion* in 1817–1818 shortly after his sister's death, Henry Austen writes that "so much did she shrink from notoriety, that no accumulation of fame would have induced her, had she lived, to affix her name to any productions of her pen."[5] Henry sought to keep his sister's good reputation intact even as he revealed her name at last as the author of the novels that were so very well regarded.

In his "Memoir of Miss Austen," written several years later, Henry concludes by saying, "Jane Austen's hopes of immortality were built upon the Rock of ages. That she deeply felt, and devoutly acknowledged, the insignificance of all worldly attainments, and the worthlessness of all human services, in the eyes of her heavenly Father."[6] It was perhaps more important to him that her devotion to her Christian faith be highlighted and remembered longer than her sharp eye and keen wit that revealed so much of the hypocrisy she saw around her.

Later, other family members wrote similar accounts that romanticized the author to varying degrees. These include *A Memoir of Jane Austen* (1871) by her nephew, James Edward Austen-Leigh. This book was expanded in 1913 by James Edward's grandson, Richard Arthur Austen-Leigh, into

Cassandra Austen, whose silhouette is seen here, devoted herself to shaping and maintaining her sister's reputation after her death in 1817.

another book published with his uncle, William Austen-Leigh, called *Jane Austen: Her Life and Letters, A Family Record.* "Recollections of Aunt Jane" (1864) was written by her niece, Anna Lefroy. Caroline Austen wrote about her great-aunt in *My Aunt Jane Austen: A Memoir* (1867).

Interest in accounts of Jane Austen's life continued into the twentieth century. Robert Chapman published an edited version of James Edward Austen-Leigh's *Memoir* in 1926. Others began studying the Austen family as well and collected their papers and life stories alongside Jane's, hoping these tales might illuminate unanswered questions about the author's life and innermost thoughts. Letters and documents passed down through the large Austen family and their descendants surfaced over time and were published and added to the record. There are still thought to be papers and records related to the author and her family that may be held in private hands.

Studies of Austen

Feminist and other late-twentieth-century scholars, critics, and readers have worked to uncover more of what the "real" Jane Austen was like. There is a desire to bring facts about the author out from under the layers of protective prose given to her memory by biased memoirists and early biographers. Two biographical accounts include *Jane Austen: A Family Record* by Deidre Le Faye (1989, 2004) and *Jane Austen: A Life* by Claire Tomalin (1997). The former account expands on Richard and William Austen-Leigh's 1913 *Life and Letters.* It continues the detailed factual record culled from extensive research of people, places, dates, and events. Tomalin's book uses much of the information from Le Faye's but is written in a narrative and more interpretive style that attempts to make observations about the effects of these facts on the author and her writing.

In 2001, Canadian author Carol Shields wrote *Jane Austen*, a narrated account of Austen's life from the viewpoint of a fellow writer. In it, she argues that Austen was not a reclusive spinster as early versions of her life story portray but was rather a writer fully engaged with the historical implications of her day. Shields writes:

> By indirection, by assumption, by reading what is implicit, we can find behind Austen's novels a steady, intelligent witness to a world that was rapidly reinventing itself. Every Austen conversation, every chance encounter on a muddy road, every evening of cards before the fire, every bold, disruptive militiaman is backed by historical implication. For even the most casual reader, the period of Austen's life, 1775–1817, becomes visible through her trenchant, knowing glance. That glance may be hard-edged or soft, part of a novel's texture or backdrop, or it may constitute the raw energy of propulsion. It is never accidental. For the biographer, one such "glance" is multiplied a thousand times. Austen's short life may have been lived in relative privacy, but her novels show her to be a citizen, and certainly a spectator, of a far wider world.[7]

In 2014, biographer Paula Byrne set out to take a fresh look at the author's life. In *The Real Jane Austen: A Life in Small Things*, Byrne says her effort was to write "something different and more experimental" than the accounts of facts from cradle to grave that have been written before. Instead, her biography "focuses on a variety of key moments, scenes, and objects" in Austen's life and work.[8] The "small things" discussed include items like an East Indian shawl, vellum notebooks, a cocked hat, a card of lace, an ivory miniature, velvet cushions, and a box of letters, among others.

In addition to biographical studies, literary critics and scholars have read and reread each of the six major novels, as well as the juvenilia, letters, and other works. Over the years, articles and books about Austen's titles and about her work collectively have become nearly an industry in themselves. Some studies attempt to place Austen's work within the context of literature or the other arts of her time. Others attempt to explain her times in more detail to give a fuller context for Austen readers. A few of these later books in Austen studies are: *What Matters in Jane Austen? Twenty Crucial Puzzles Solved* (2014) by John Mullen; *Jane Austen's Names: Riddles, Persons, Places* (2014) by Margaret Doody; *Jane Austen's England* (2013) by Roy Adkins and Lesley Adkins; *What Would Jane Do? Quips and Wisdom from Jane Austen* (2014) designed by Potter Style; *A Truth Universally Acknowledged: 33 Great Writers on Why We Read Jane Austen* (2010), edited by Susannah Carson and Harold Bloom; *Jane Austen and the Romantic Poets* (2004) by William Deresiewicz; *Jane Austen and the Theatre* (2006) by Penny Gay; *Jane Austen and the Fiction of Her Time* (1999) by Mary Waldron; and *Jane Austen, Women, Politics, and the Novel* (1988) by Claudia L. Johnson.

Because she lived at home and wrote about the seemingly mundane details of everyday life, many readers believe that "finding the real Jane Austen," or what she really felt and thought about certain subjects not alluded to in her novels or letters, may be an exercise in futility. Nevertheless, fascination with any new biographical discovery, literary interpretation, or historical and cultural contexts remains high for scholars as well as general readers and Austen fans around the world.

Austen in Film and Television

Austen's legacy extends beyond the pages of biographies and literary criticism. Both film and television have embraced her life and work, bringing her biography and stories to an even wider audience. Many films and television programs have been adapted from her novels. There always seems to be a new adaptation in the works.

One of the earliest film adaptations of an Austen novel was a fifty-five-minute black-and-white version of *Pride and Prejudice* adapted by Michael Barry. Laurence Olivier played Mr. Darcy in a 1940 film adaptation of the same novel. *Sense and Sensibility* was run on British television as a miniseries of four, forty-five-minute episodes in 1971. It was remade into a feature film in the 1995 screenplay by actress Emma Thompson. In 2002, a television documentary, *The Real Jane Austen*, was produced in the United Kingdom.[9] Perhaps the most well-known and beloved of the Austen adaptations is the 1995 BBC *Pride and Prejudice* miniseries starring Jennifer Ehle as Elizabeth and Colin Firth as Mr. Darcy.

Film and television have not limited themselves to adaptations of Austen novels. Austen has inspired a growth beyond her covers in what writers for visual media wish to do. Examples are many; just as many may raise eyebrows among the Austen faithful. Some film and television titles in this vein include *Austenland* (2013); *Emma Approved* (2013); *The Lizzie Bennet Diaries* (2012); *The Jane Austen Book Club* (2007); *Lost in Austen* (2008); and *Becoming Jane* (2007) starring Anne Hathaway.

Jane Austen: The Image, the Icon

Jane Austen has become an icon not only in literature and film but also in popular culture. As is customary with any icon,

Austen's popularity in this area began with an image. Around 1810, her sister, Cassandra, sketched Jane in pencil and watercolor but never finished the portrait. It is the only known, authenticated image of her face drawn from life. Cassandra also painted a watercolor of Jane from the back around 1804. Jane is depicted sitting on the ground near a tree, apparently looking out at something, perhaps a seaside scene. She is wearing a blue dress and bonnet with ribbons dangling in the breeze.

Around 1869, James Andrews of Maidenhead painted a watercolor miniature of Austen derived from Cassandra's 1810 sketch. For the frontispiece to his *Memoir*, James Edward

Anne Hathaway stars in *Becoming Jane*, a fictionalized account of Austen's love life.

While there exist several images reported to be of Jane Austen, Cassandra Austen's watercolor miniature of her sister is the only image that is known to be authentic.

Austen-Leigh commissioned Scottish artist William Home Lizars to create a steel engraving from Andrews's watercolor.[10] The engraving, in particular, is frequently reprinted on items for sale, such as T-shirts, tote bags, coffee mugs, and so forth. A black profile silhouette also frequently used in popular culture to represent the author may or may not be that of Jane Austen.

To the Janeites and others interested in the author, her work, and her times, Jane Austen represents more than a brilliant nineteenth-century British author. She represents a time and culture gone long before the days of the Internet, cell phones, laptop computers, and downloads. For many, Austen provides nostalgia for days gone by or a window into history. For others, she offers close examinations of human relationships that are as fresh, true, witty, and revealing today as they were two hundred years ago.

Remotely Austen?

If film, television, and silhouetted images of Austen on T-shirts, book bags, and coffee mugs seem to be moving her further and further away from her novels, new books are now appearing that ironically do the same. More recently, there have been a series of books and affiliated projects that have claimed Jane Austen as an inspiration, influence, or her work as perhaps the mere starting place for an idea. Sometimes, true fans of the author's novels question the validity of these claims; other times, readers enjoy the playfulness that Austen's work seems to engender in other writers and artists.

For example, in 2009, a parody of *Pride and Prejudice* called *Pride and Prejudice and Zombies* written by Seth Grahame-Smith was published. Essentially, the book is a "mash-up" of the novel with fiction about zombies mixed into it. It credits

Austen as co-author. While some critics praised the book for aiding modern audiences in appreciating Austen's use of words in a new way, others panned the project. The book was so successful, however, that a prequel by Steve Hockensmith called *Pride and Prejudice and Zombies: Dawn of the Dreadfuls*, and his sequel, *Pride and Prejudice and Zombies: Dreadfully Ever After*, appeared in 2010 and 2011, respectively.

Not only were there additional titles to the zombie book published, but spin-off projects to it appeared as well. These include a video game, an interactive e-book, and a graphic novel (*Pride and Prejudice and Zombies: The Graphic Novel*). In 2016, a feature film of the zombie version of *Pride and Prejudice* was released in theaters with a screenplay by Burr Steers. Actor Lily James plays Elizabeth Bennet while Sam Riley plays Mr. Darcy. One of the film's producers is Academy Award-winning actor Natalie Portman. So, not only has Austen's novel created a zombie book adaptation, but that zombie book has, in turn, spun off its own adaptations in gaming and in film.

Another example of books remotely affiliated with Austen are series of novels that "retell" her stories, or spin-off Austen characters into new stories, or base characters on Austen-related figures, or employ Austen settings. Examples of these include an Amish version of *Sense and Sensibility*; mysteries called *Being a Jane Austen Mystery*; and a *Jane Austen Academy* series that calls itself "Austenesque." Famed mystery author P.D. James' final novel was a "sequel" to *Pride & Prejudice* titled *Death Comes to Pemberly.* The novel was a murder mystery in which Elizabeth Bennet (now Darcy) has to solce the mystery of a family members' death. It was adapted by the BBC into a miniseries in 2013.

Still other books launch from Jane Austen into books about the author and something else—Jane Austen and food, dances in Austen's time, fashion from the novels, gardening, and just about any "Austen and *fill in the blank subject*" someone might find interesting to explore.

Yet another "remote" use of Austen is in social media on the Internet. Twitter, for example, has several accounts devoted to the author. Some are associated with Austen sites in Great Britain or academic study; others are created by readers and fans. Some Twitter handles related to the author include: @JaneAustenLIVES (nearly seventeen thousand followers); @JaneAustenBath (six thousand followers); and @pemberleydotcom (almost seven thousand followers).

Austen's most enthusiastic fans, known as Janeites, are devoted to all aspects of the novelist's life and times. As seen here, they often participate in balls, tea parties, readings, or other activities while dressed in period costume.

On Facebook, Jane Austen has a verified page. It is maintained by the US and UK Viking publishers of her books. The Jane Austen House Museum in Chawton has its own Facebook page as does the Jane Austen Centre in Bath. On Pinterest, nearly seven hundred pins with approximately fifteen hundred followers feature Austen-related quotes, posters, book covers, baked goods, postage stamps, movie stills, and more.

Austen In and Out of the Classroom

academics

Academics are people involved with formal education. They include professors, teachers, and students as well as school administrators.

Though she lived long ago and in a different era, another testament to Austen's endurance in world literature and culture is that the relevance and popularity of her work appears to have increased with time. Colleges and high schools consistently assign Austen's works to today's students to read, discuss, and write about. Scholars hold meetings and conferences about her work, continually sharing new research and critical interpretations. The Modern Language Association (MLA), a global organization dedicated to the teaching and study of language and literature, cites approximately three thousand books and articles related to Jane Austen in its *International Bibliography*.

Appreciation of the author extends outside the classroom as well. The Jane Austen Society was established in the United Kingdom in 1940. It is made up of both academics and non-academics who wish to promote the reading, enjoyment, and study of the author. Two other large societies dedicated to the author have been established around the world. They are the Jane Austen Society of North America (JASNA), founded in 1979, and the Jane Austen Society of Australia (JASA) in 1989.

To the disturbance or delight of many of her serious readers, Jane Austen's popularity in recent times has made her an icon in popular culture. Many Janeites even gather together to dress in period clothing, play games from Austen's time such as whist, answer quizzes based on minutia from the novels, and have teas and discuss gardening and other topics related to life in Austen's time. Whether it is through the quiet appreciation of a witty turn of phrase in an Austen novel or a group trip organized to follow in Austen's footsteps around various sites in England, there is no doubt that the study and appreciation of Jane Austen is alive and well.

CHRONOLOGY

1775– Jane Austen is born on December 16 in Steventon, Hampshire.

1801– Austen family moves to Bath, Somerset.

1805– Austen's father dies in Bath.

1806–1809– Visits for long stays with brothers and others.

1809– Moves with mother and sister to Chawton Cottage, Hampshire.

1811– *Sense and Sensibility* is published.

1813– *Pride and Prejudice* is published.

1814– *Mansfield Park* is published.

1815–1816– *Emma* is published, dedicated to the Prince Regent.

1817– On July 18, Jane Austen dies in Winchester and is buried in Winchester Cathedral on July 24; in December, *Northanger Abbey* and *Persuasion* are published.

1833– Richard Bentley publishes the collected works of Jane Austen. Her novels have never gone out of print from that day forward.

1871– J. E. Austen-Leigh, the author's nephew, publishes *A Memoir of Jane Austen.* The biography and memoir aid in launching what would become Austen's lasting fame and legacy in world literature.

1884– Selection of Austen's surviving letters published, edited by Baron Brabourne.

1932– More comprehensive edition of Austen's letters published, edited by R. W. Chapman.

1940– Jane Austen Society of the United Kingdom is founded by Dorothy Darnell with an initial goal of preserving Chawton Cottage.

1979– Jane Austen Society of North America is founded by Joan Austen-Leigh (great-great grand-niece of Austen), Henry G. Burke, and J. David Grey.

2011– *Sense and Sensibility: The Bath Bicentenary Edition* is published.

2011– Fourth comprehensive edition of Jane Austen's letters is published, including new scholarship and annotations, edited by Deirdre Le Faye.

2013– Austen fans around the world celebrate *Pride and Prejudice* publication bicentennial with readings, exhibits, costumed events, and more.

2015–2016– Austen enthusiasts celebrate the bicentennial of *Emma*'s publication.

Chapter Notes

Chapter 1. Working a Fine Brush on Ivory

1. Deirdre Le Faye, *Jane Austen: A Family Record* (Cambridge: Cambridge University Press, 2004), xviii–xxix.
2. Letter to James Edward Austen, December 16–17, 1816; Jane Austen, *Jane Austen's Letters*, 3rd ed., collected and edited by Deirdre Le Faye (Oxford: Oxford University Press, 1997), p. 323.
3. "A First Appearance," *The Rudyard Kipling Collection*, Cushing Memorial Library and Archives, Texas A&M University, archiveexhibits.library.tamu.edu/kipling/story.html (accessed Nov. 8, 2015).
4. Rudyard Kipling, "The Janeites," *Debts and Credits* (Garden City, NY: Doubleday, Page & Company, 1926), p. 124–147.
5. Ibid.
6. Ibid.
7. Ibid.
8. Deborah Yaffe, *Among the Janeites* (New York: Houghton Mifflin Harcourt, 2013), xiv.

Chapter 2. The Life and Times of Georgian and Regency England

1. "George IV," *Historic Figures*, BBC Online, www.bbc.co.uk/history/historic_figures/george_iv_king.shtml (accessed Nov. 8, 2015).
2. Paula Byrne, *The Real Jane Austen: A Life in Small Things* (New York: HarperCollins, 2014), p. 297–299.
3. Daniel Pool, *What Jane Austen Ate and Charles Dickens Knew: From Fox Hunting to Whist—The Facts of Daily Life in 19th-Century England* (New York: Simon & Schuster, 1994), p. 163.

4. Kirstin Olsen, *All Things Austen: An Encyclopedia of Austen's World* (Westport, Conn.: Greenwood Press, 2005), p. 324–325.
5. Pool, p. 54–55.
6. Ibid., p. 55–56.
7. Olsen, p. 144.
8. Pool, p. 72–85.
9. Ibid., p. 72–78.
10. Ibid., p. 78–81.
11. Letter to Cassandra Austen, November 25, 1798; Jane Austen, *Jane Austen's Letters*, 4th ed., collected and edited by Deirdre Le Faye (Oxford: Oxford University Press, 2011), p. 22.
12. Olsen, p. 201.
13. Pool, p. 343.
14. Olsen, p. 200–201.
15. Pool, p. 82–83.

Chapter 3. Literature in Austen's Time

1. "Picaresque novel," *Encyclopedia Britannica*, 2015, www.britannica.com/eb/article-9059900/picaresque-novel (accessed Nov. 8, 2015).
2. "Gothic novel," *Encyclopedia Britannica*, 2015, www.britannica.com/eb/article-9037491/Gothic-novel (accessed Nov. 8, 2015).
3. "Epistolary novel," *Encyclopedia Britannica*, 2015, www.britannica.com/eb/article-9032818/epistolary-novel (accessed Nov. 8, 2015).
4. Mary Lascelles, *Jane Austen and Her Art* (London: Athlone, 2002), p. 202–203.

5. Letter to Anna Austen, August 10, 1914; Jane Austen, *Jane Austen's Letters*, 4th ed., collected and edited by Deirdre Le Faye (Oxford: Oxford University Press, 2011), p. 269.
6. John F. Burrows, "Style," *The Cambridge Companion to Jane Austen*, Edward Copeland and Juliet McMaster, eds. (Cambridge: Cambridge University Press, 1997), p. 178.

Chapter 4. An Unsettled Life

1. Deirdre Le Faye, *Jane Austen: A Family Record* (Cambridge: Cambridge University Press, 2004), xviii–xxix.
2. Claire Tomalin, *Jane Austen: A Life* (New York: Vintage, 1999), p. 8.
3. Le Faye, *Jane Austen: A Family Record*, p. 49.
4. Deirdre Le Faye, *Jane Austen's Country Life* (London: Frances Lincoln, 2014), p. 50–52.
5. Le Faye, *Jane Austen: A Family Record*, p. 57.
6. Ibid., p. 57–59.
7. Carol Shields, *Jane Austen* (New York: Penguin, 2005), p. 23–24.
8. Ibid., p. 32.
9. Claire Harman, *Jane's Fame* (New York: Henry Holt, 2009), p. 6.
10. Shields, p. 35.
11. Harman, p. 20–21.
12. Anne-Marie Edwards, *In the Steps of Jane Austen* (Madison, WI: Jones Books, 2003), p. 75–99.
13. Tomalin, p. 210.
14. Edwards, p. 133.

Chapter 5. The First: *Sense and Sensibility*

1. Deirdre Le Faye, *Jane Austen: A Family Record* (Cambridge: Cambridge University Press, 2004), xxi–xxvi.

2. Mary Favret, "*Sense and Sensibility*: The Letter, Post Factum," *Sense and Sensibility*, Norton Critical Edition, Claudia L. Johnson, ed. (New York: W. W. Norton, 2002), p. 373.
3. Paul Poplawski, "*Sense and Sensibility*," *A Jane Austen Encyclopedia* (Westport, Conn.: Greenwood Press, 1998), p. 268.
4. Ibid., p. 269.
5. Mary Poovey, "Ideological Contradictions and the Consolations of Form: *Sense and Sensibility*," *Sense and Sensibility*, Norton Critical Edition, Claudia L. Johnson, ed. (New York: W. W. Norton, 2002), p. 338.
6. Gene Ruoff, "Wills," *Sense and Sensibility*, Norton Critical Edition, Claudia L. Johnson, ed. (New York: W. W. Norton, 2002), p. 348.
7. Jane Austen, "Contexts," *Sense and Sensibility*, Norton Critical Edition, Claudia L. Johnson, ed. (New York: W. W. Norton, 2002), p. 273–291.
8. *Sense and Sensibility* (film), *Internet Movie Database*, www.imdb.com/title/tt0114388/ (accessed Nov. 8, 2015).
9. Claudia L. Johnson, *Jane Austen: Women, Politics, and the Novel* (Chicago: University of Chicago Press, 1990), p. 55–58.
10. Jan Fergus, "First Publication," *Sense and Sensibility*, Norton Critical Edition, Claudia L. Johnson, ed. (New York: W. W. Norton, 2002), p. 331.
11. Ibid.

Chapter 6. The Classic: *Pride and Prejudice*

1. Jane Austen, "*Pride and Prejudice*," *The Oxford Illustrated Jane Austen*, 3rd ed. (Oxford: Oxford University Press, 1988), vol. 2, p. 3.

2. Austen, *Pride and Prejudice*, p. 13.
3. Mary Lascelles, *Jane Austen and Her Art* (London: Athlone, 2002), p. 160–163.
4. Letter to Cassandra Austen, January 29, 1813; Jane Austen, *Jane Austen's Letters*, 4th ed., collected and edited by Deirdre Le Faye (Oxford: Oxford University Press, 2011), p. 201.
5. Ibid.
6. Deirdre Le Faye, *Jane Austen: A Family Record* (Cambridge: Cambridge University Press, 2004), p. 195.
7. Ibid., p. 196.
8. Letter to Cassandra Austen, February 4, 1813; Jane Austen, *Jane Austen's Letters*, 4th ed., collected and edited by Deirdre Le Faye (Oxford: Oxford University Press, 2011), p. 203.
9. James Sherry, "*Pride and Prejudice*: The Limits of Society," *Studies in English Literature, 1500–1900* 19, no. 4 (Autumn 1979): 612.
10. Marilyn Butler, "Jane Austen and the War of Ideas," *Pride and Prejudice*, Norton Critical Edition, Donald Gray, ed. (New York: W. W. Norton), p. 321.

Chapter 7. A Problematic Novel: *Mansfield Park*

1. Jane Austen, "Opinions of *Mansfield Park*," *Mansfield Park*, Norton Critical Edition, Claudia L. Johnson, ed. (New York: W. W. Norton & Co., 1998), p. 376–377.
2. "Opinions of *Mansfield Park*," *The Republic of Pemberley*, www.pemberley.com/janeinfo/opmansfp.html (accessed Nov. 8, 2015).
3. Lionel Trilling, "*Mansfield Park*," *The Opposing Self: Nine Essays on Criticism* (1955; reprint, New York: Viking Press, 1959), p. 212.

4. Jane Austen, "*Mansfield Park*," *Oxford Illustrated Jane Austen* (Oxford: Oxford University Press, 1988), p. 3.
5. Natalie Tyler, *The Friendly Jane Austen* (New York: Penguin, 1999), p. 143.
6. C. S. Lewis, "A Note on Jane Austen," *Jane Austen: A Collection of Critical Essays*, ed. Ian Watt (Englewood Cliffs, N.J.: Prentice-Hall, 1963), p. 25–34.
7. Amy J. Pawl, "Fanny Price and the Sentimental Genealogy of *Mansfield Park*," *Eighteenth-Century Fiction* 16, no. 2 (January 2004): 288.
8. Christopher Lyndon, "J. K. Rowling Interview Transcript," *The Connection* (WBUR Radio), October 12, 1999.
9. John Wiltshire, "*Mansfield Park, Emma, Persuasion*," *The Cambridge Companion to Jane Austen*, Edward Copeland and Juliet McMaster, eds. (Cambridge: Cambridge University Press, 2003), p. 61.
10. Ibid., p. 65.
11. Mary Lascelles, *Jane Austen and Her Art* (London: Athlone, 2002), p. 35.

Chapter 8. "Perfect" *Emma*

1. Jane Austen, "*Emma*," *The Oxford Illustrated Jane Austen*, 3rd ed. (Oxford: Oxford University Press, 1988), pp. 4–5.
2. Paul Poplawski, "*Emma*," *A Jane Austen Encyclopedia* (Westport, CT: Greenwood Press, 1998), p. 129–130.
3. Deirdre Le Faye, *Jane Austen: A Family Record* (Cambridge: Cambridge University Press, 2004), p. 232.
4. Poplawski, p. 130.
5. "Sir Walter Scott," *Encyclopedia Britannica*, http://www.britannica.com/biography/Sir-Walter-Scott-1st-Baronet (accessed Nov. 8, 2015).

6. Letter from James Stanier Clarke to Jane Austen, November 16, 1815; *Jane Austen's Letters*, 4th ed., collected and edited by Deirdre Le Faye (Oxford: Oxford University Press, 2011), p. 296.
7. Letter to John Murray, December 11, 1815; *Jane Austen's Letters*, 4th ed., collected and edited by Deirdre Le Faye (Oxford: Oxford University Press, 2011), p. 304.
8. Jane Austen, "*Emma*," *The Oxford Illustrated Jane Austen*, 3rd ed. (Oxford: Oxford University Press, 1988), p. 4.
9. John Wiltshire, "*Mansfield Park, Emma, Persuasion*," *The Cambridge Companion to Jane Austen*, Edward Copeland and Juliet McMaster, eds. (Cambridge: Cambridge University Press, 2003), p. 75.

Chapter 9. Juvenilia and Posthumous Works

1. A. S. Byatt, "Introduction," *The History of England by a partial, prejudiced, & ignorant Historian*, by Jane Austen, a complete facsimile of the original text, with illustrations by her sister Cassandra (Chapel Hill, NC: Algonquin Books of Chapel Hill, 1993), vi.
2. Jane Austen, *Catharine and Other Writings* (Oxford: Oxford University Press, 1993), p. 135.
3. Jane Austen, *Catharine*, vii–viii.
4. Ibid., p. 237.
5. Letter to Crosby and Co., April 5, 1809; *Jane Austen's Letters*, 4th ed., collected and edited by Deirdre Le Faye (Oxford: Oxford University Press, 2011), p. 174–175.
6. Jan Fergus, "The Professional Woman Writer," *The Cambridge Companion to Jane Austen*, Edward Copeland and Juliet McMaster, eds. (Cambridge: Cambridge University Press, 1997), p. 12.

7. Jane Austen, *Lady Susan/The Watsons/Sanditon*, edited with an introduction by Margaret Drabble (New York: Penguin, 1974).

Chapter 10. Austen's Legacy

1. Claire Tomalin, *Jane Austen: A Life* (New York: Vintage, 1999), p. 260.
2. Ibid., p. 283.
3. Ibid., p. 285.
4. Josephine Ross, *Jane Austen: A Companion* (New Brunswick, NJ: Rutgers University Press, 2002), illustration no. 44.
5. Henry Austen, "Biographical Notice of the Author," *A Memoir of Jane Austen and Other Family Recollections*, Kathyrn Sutherland, ed. (Oxford: Oxford University Press, 2002), p. 140.
6. Henry Austen, "Memoir of Miss Austen," *A Memoir of Jane Austen and Other Family Recollections*, Kathyrn Sutherland, ed. (Oxford: Oxford University Press, 2002), p. 153.
7. Carol Shields, *Jane Austen* (New York: Penguin, 2001), p. 4.
8. Paula Byrne, *The Real Jane Austen: A Life in Small Things* (New York: Harper, 2014), p. 6.
9. "Jane Austen, Writer," *Internet Movie Database*, www.imdb.com/name/nm0000807 (accessed Nov. 8, 2015).
10. Deirdre Le Faye, *Jane Austen: A Family Record* (Cambridge: Cambridge University Press, 2004), p. 83.

Literary Terms

dialogue—Characters' speech in fiction.

domestic novel—A novel in which the primary setting is the home and the main characters are from a family.

epistolary novel—A novel written in the form of letters between two or more characters.

exposition—Narration, explanation, or description in fiction.

gothic novel—A novel in which a female character is taken into hiding in a dungeon, castle, and so forth and usually rescued by a male hero.

irony—The incongruity of an expected situation (or its outcome) and the actual situation (or its outcome). In language, irony is a figure of speech that says one thing but means another. In comic irony, this disconnect creates a humorous, sarcastic (or mocking) effect.

juvenilia—An author's childhood writing or writing done while a teenager.

metafiction—Self-conscious storytelling that brings attention to its own composition or elements.

omniscient point of view—A "godlike" narrator that tells the story and can tell what characters are thinking.

picaresque novel—One in which a rogue character gets through one adventure after another on his charm and wits.

plot—A planned sequence of events in fiction.

point of view—The perspective from which a story is told.

protagonist—The main character of a story or novel.

realistic fiction—The opposite of fantasy, this is a story written as though it could really happen, in a setting that actually existed or could exist.

setting—The time, place, and culture in which a story or novel takes place.

tone—The writer's attitude toward her subject or audience.

Works by Jane Austen

Major Works

Sense and Sensibility (1811)
Pride and Prejudice (1813)
Mansfield Park (1814)
Emma (1815–1816)
Northanger Abbey (1817)
Persuasion (1817)

Minor Works

Juvenilia (Volumes I, II, III)
Lady Susan
The Watsons
Sanditon (incomplete)

Further Reading

Adkins, Roy, and Lesley Adkins. *Jane Austen's England: Daily Life in the Georgian and Regency Periods.* New York: Penguin, 2014.

Bloom, Harold, ed. *Jane Austen (Bloom's Modern Critical Views).* Philadelphia: Chelsea House, 2009.

Jenkyns, Richard. *A Fine Brush on Ivory: An Appreciation of Jane Austen.* Oxford: Oxford University Press, 2007.

Le Faye, Deirdre, ed. *Jane Austen's Letters.* New York: Oxford University Press, 2011.

Locke, Juliane. *England's Jane: The Story of Jane Austen.* Greensboro, NC: Morgan Reynolds, 2006.

Poplawski, Paul. *A Jane Austen Encyclopedia.* Westport, CT: Greenwood Press, 1998.

Todd, Janet. *Jane Austen: Her Life, Her Times, Her Novels.* London: Andre Deutsch, 2014.

Websites

The Jane Austen Information Page
www.pemberley.com/janeinfo/janeinfo.html
Includes text of novels and minor works, biography, and miscellaneous Austen-related articles.

Jane Austen Society of North America (JASNA) Home Page
www.jasna.org/
Stay up to date on all things Austen and join in discussions about the writer and her works.

Jane Austen Society of the United Kingdom
www.janeaustensoci.freeuk.com/#
Delve into Austen's writings and learn more about her life and the time in which she lived.

Index